ABBADON

Megan Hernandez never planned to become one of a very few
female serial killers. She had killed for a living in a secret
special forces division, but that was much different.

That was her job, this would be her calling!

C. C. Chamberlane

Abbadon

C. C. Chamberlane

Published by C. C. Chamberlane, 2022.

ABBADON

First edition. February 16, 2022.

ISBN: 978-1775373209

Written by C. C. Chamberlane.

Also by C. C. Chamberlane

Megan Hernandez
Samaela
The First Female Navy SEAL
Saving Ukraine

Standalone
Abbadon

ABBADON
C. C. CHAMBERLANE

Megan Hernandez had not planned to become one of the small percentage of serial killers who happen to be female.
In fact, she had fought evil a good deal of her life and had served her country with honor and distinction. It was all top-secret, but she knew she had done what her country required of her.
All it took was one boyfriend being abusive to set her on this path to protect all women from jerks like him...
If you have comments or ideas, please email us directly at
CCChamberlane@gmail.com
@ccchamberlane

ABBADON

ISBN Print – 978-1-7753732-0-9

Copyright 2018 C. C. CHAMBERLANE

Published by Stephen Mackisoc (Author) All rights to any publication, in whole or in part, remain the sole property of Stephen Mackisoc.

Acknowledgements
This book would not have been published without the advice, proofreading skills and comments from Jennifer, Susan and Kaylyn. All of them helped ensure the overall quality of this book and I appreciate their effort.

About the Author – C.C. Chamberlane

This is the first fact-influenced-fiction crime novel in a series that will feature the work of Megan Hernandez. I really hope you enjoy this book and will watch for the next adventure. Follow her exploits as she makes the world a better place.

I have always been a true crime type person as these stories are multi-layered and stimulate deep thought. I find both the character development and plot development fascinating and have always been a fan.

After reading ABBADON, you can follow Meg Hernandez and Norie on their next adventure, SAMAELA. Keep an eye on our Facebook page at C.C.Chamberlane and watch for the next title in the series.

Prologue

Megan Hernandez, or Meg as her friends always called her, was destined for something in the military or law enforcement from the day she was born. Her father and grandfather were both skilled military men and her mother was a decorated detective. She was always fascinated by the stories each person would tell about their exploits, challenges and accomplishments. As she grew older, the stories and lessons to be learned around the dinner table helped shape who she would become.

Meg was never encumbered by any thoughts about girls being "weaker" or less important than boys. The concept was completely foreign to everyone she knew and grew up with. Her whole family ensured that she knew equality was built into her DNA. She excelled in all aspects of her training once she entered the military. Megan was frequently recognized as top of class. She was never sure why she went the direction she did, but Megan knew she was making a real difference once she finally found her true calling after her discharge.

She started dating a fellow a couple of years after her release, and things were good at first. They took a turn down a bad path early in the relationship and, being who she was, Meg was not about to put up with any abuse. She knew she couldn't simply kill her abusive boyfriend. Well, she was certainly capable of it, but she would need to be incredibly careful.

She considered poison, cutting the brake lines, tons of ideas went through her head. She was a trained killer however, so she knew that any of those methods would likely land her in a prison. The spouse/partner was always the first place they looked, and poison was a frequent weapon of choice in these cases.

No, this had to be a very well thought-out and comprehensive plan. She set about designing one and then putting it into action.

Meg had no idea THIS would soon become what she would accept as her life's work.

Chapter One – Background

I had a short but distinguished career in a little-known special forces division. In fact, it was even less than little-known, it was top-secret. Even the President didn't know about me or the others on my team. We operated in the dark alleys and seedy underbelly of our government. We never showed up in the news and deaths of targets or agents were never published. Our instructions were not known to politicians as they could never truly be trusted to keep a secret. Once recruited onto the team we never met our handlers. They too operated in anonymity just like the people whose lives and actions they directed. That was just the way it had to be to ensure everyone involved in the program was protected.

Due to my unique talents, athletic ability and the fact I was somewhat easy on the eyes, I was a deadly combination. I excelled at my job. I performed so well that after only eight years I was given a full discharge. My short career bought me a lifelong pension that was more than enough to keep me housed, clothed and fed until I died.

At age 36, a little more than $5,000 a month with complete and comprehensive medical coverage included was a rather good deal. Due to my service, it was also tax-free income! It was more than I had made on active duty, risking my life on every assignment. Nobody knew anything of this history, and I was never about to let anyone know.

I really made a solid attempt to just live off the radar. When I was discharged, I just wanted to relax and enjoy the type of life I saw those around me living. There are people who were not constantly on edge and living a kill or be killed existence. I envied them. I was excited about my next life and anxious to get it started.

I knew I needed to have a solid backstory to protect my identity. I didn't want anyone discovering what I used to do. As far as anyone was concerned, I had worked as a fact checker and background person for a newspaper. If money ever came up the story would be I had inherited a good deal of money from my Aunt. I would say she had purchased annuities for me that were allowing me to live out a happy life. I had the facts and figures of the story all dialed in, so it was unlikely I would ever slip up and give myself away. Besides, most of that story was true. What kept me alive this long was just such attention to detail. I would have to keep that my whole life.

I thought the story made sense. I did have a deceased rich aunt to back it up and it explained the healthy "pension" I was receiving from my time in the military. It was also my aunt who had left me the house in which I now lived. I wasn't sure if this so-called pension was a reward or just hush-money, but I had no plans to tell anyone anything. I was going to collect my cash until the day I died and that was that. I had earned that money doing things I still lose sleep over to this day. I knew I was acting in the best interests of my country, but it still weighed heavily on me.

I met Bobby about two years after I was discharged. I had gotten over the work I had been doing and settled into a safe, suburban lifestyle. I had a couple of girlfriends I had met, and we spent a good deal of time together.

I met them both at the gym I trained at and we just kind of clicked right out of the gate.

Kathy and Angela were both gorgeous and I figured they had rich old sugar daddies funding their lifestyle. They were very nice and fun to be around though. They were the first "girl friends" I had had in years. Up until my discharge I was always hanging around with the guys. I felt like I fit in better, much the same as cops tend to enjoy other cops, firefighters spend time with other firefighters etc. The shared experiences are a very solid connection that make those personal bonds tougher to break.

Because of getting to know Kathy and Angie, I was able to get over my own bias about women who seemed incapable of taking care of themselves. I realized that I looked down my nose at women like that, so I worked hard to alter my perspective. Just because I loved the way I lived and who I was did not mean it was the ONLY way.

At first, I didn't think we would have a connection as they were both married to rich men and seemed to enjoy the lifestyle that came with that.

I thought I had seen that type before. I was very wrong and quickly found out that, like me, they were accomplished athletes in college and truly their own women. Other than what I had done in the past for employment we did have quite a bit in common.

We all became friends quickly and that really helped me to adjust to civilian life better. I really believed that I was slowly getting over my past and I was starting to relax and enjoy life. I wasn't having many nightmares these days nor was I constantly on edge any longer. It was good to think I might be getting over the terrible things I had seen and done. It made me feel that I was making progress toward living that normal life I thought I wanted.

It took a long while to begin to get over those feelings. When your life is in danger 100% of the time you learn to think and react very fast. You were wary of everyone and everything around you, it was the only way to stay alive. We were trained to look at the world through a much different set of lenses than "regular" people do. This training then colored every part of your life. Thanks to that extensive and complex training I had made the right decisions in life-threatening situations almost every time.

I completely understand how today's forces people struggle with PTSD when they return home. They were usually more on the front lines than I was and had to deal with things like IED's and everything else that comes with being a soldier.

They do not receive the type of pension and medical coverage that I enjoy either.

Imagine if, at your job, each time someone approached you in the office, on the street, in the washroom or at the bank there was a chance they were going to try and kill you? It might be a child, a teenager, a grandmother; you simply never knew from where the threat might come.

They could use a gun, a knife, poison or they could even be a suicide bomber. At least my Grandfather KNEW who the enemy was when he was in the war. It was the guy pointing a rifle at him from the foxhole less than 100 yards away! There were times a grenade would land in the trench, and someone would just pick it up and toss it back over. Different times!

It was no easier on them to shoot and kill people they might have otherwise had a beer with, but it was their job. My grandfather's stories tended to be more about the humour surrounding what they had to do as young men. I think that was a Canadian thing as he lived in Newfoundland after emigrating from Scotland and was fighting for the Canadian army. Those folks could see humour in just about anything it seemed.

My favorite story of his was a description of a battlefield "emergency" he encountered.

As a sniper, he and his spotter were always in the trenches before dawn. Your eyes are well-rested, and your vision is excellent as the sun begins to rise. The spotter would have the picture of the selected target, typically a high-ranking leader who was still in the trenches.

They would account for wind and distance and my grandfather would make the required shot when it became available. When I asked him about it, he just said that everyone had a job to do and that was his. When all was said and done, he was quite happy to get home alive with all his body parts intact.

On this day, a corpsman came running through the trenches shouting my grandfather's name. As he got closer, my grandfather noticed he was carrying something. When he got next to him, he saw that it was his pair of soccer boots. The corpsman crouched beside him and told him that his presence was needed immediately behind the front lines. As they made their way rearward, he was shocked when he was told that a couple of colonels had arranged a soccer match between their units.

As the story goes, the Canadian Colonel and the British Colonel were sharing some whisky the previous night and the talk to turned to soccer.

It started as an innocent "my guys can beat your guys" and by morning had morphed into a full-on fight to the death on a makeshift soccer pitch.

My grandfather was an accomplished midfielder and everyone in his unit knew he was a game-changer. He always found it hilarious that he was one of the best snipers they had, he had a high value target in his sights, and the soccer game between allies took precedence.

What they did not find humour in was the equipment they were typically given to wage this battle. As far as the war went, he was an accomplished sniper who was originally equipped with the Ross rifle favored by the Canadian army. The Ross did not perform well and was quite heavy, so it fell out of favour quickly. It tended to jam and was both heavier and longer than others. It also did not handle the dirt and mud very well.

The US army had the Springfield model 1903. It was chambered in a 30.06 calibre with a five-shell magazine. It was likely the best of the three. There were many cases where Canadian soldiers would shed their Ross and grab a better rifle from a fallen comrade. The brits and some others carried the Lee-Enfield .303, and it was a much better weapon in the trenches than was the Ross. The ammunition was also interchangeable with the Ross as it too was a .303 so that made the Lee-Enfield the pickup of choice. I still have that rifle and it amazes me they could hit anything past twenty-five yards with those things.

It is all vastly different today.

Improvements in rifles, ammunition and technology have created snipers my grandfather would never have even dreamed of. Recently, a Canadian sniper bested the longest sniper shot ever recorded which was previously held by a British special forces' member. To give you an idea, Chris Kyle's longest kill shot (the film American Sniper was based on him) was 2,100 yards or 1.92 kilometres.

That mark was beaten by a British sniper in 2009 named Craig Harrison. He completed a shot at 2,640 yards or 2.475 kilometres. Harrison's mark was recently obliterated by an un-named Canadian sniper who took out an IS militant at 3,871 yards or 3.54 kilometres away!

The shot was so long he had to even consider the curvature of the earth. The projectile took almost TEN seconds to reach its target after leaving the barrel of the rifle. I think three of the current top five longest sniper shots were taken by Canadians. It seems my grandfather left a bit of a legacy. One I would come to appreciate.

Thanks to technology, people in the services today struggle to identify who exactly their enemy is and protect themselves and each other. The only way to stay alive is to be right on the edge all the time as you never know what might come at you and from where or whom it might come.

Whether you were wearing a uniform or doing what I did, you can never ever let your guard down.

The "new wars" seem so much more dangerous to me. Knowing who your enemy is now has become a combination of art and science. More often than not you need to rely on your gut instincts to quickly ascertain whether a threat is meaningful or not. You put pressure on yourself in addition to the pressure from senior officers to ensure that you make the right call.

In my case, there were generally no other lives at risk should I make a wrong decision. In reality, it was either my life or the target's and that was where it ended. In some ways it was cleaner and easier but in others it was far more complicated than it appeared.

Chapter Two – The Boys

I was now far, far away from that life and those people and stories. I was just a regular person, or as close as I could ever get to regular. I worked hard at trying to be "normal", but it was a challenge for me. For eight years my normal was waking up and planning to kill another human being.

One day at the gym Kathy told me she was having a little gathering at her place, and she asked if I wanted to come. I really didn't want to move my social life up a notch yet, but she was relentless. I could tell she was not going to give up. She said that her and Angela really wanted me to meet their husbands and their friends.

I hadn't heard too much about them other than the fact they were some sort of financial types. They really didn't share too much else, but I will admit I was somewhat intrigued. I figured I knew the type. Fat old guys who snag a young wife by giving them a lifestyle they could never otherwise have. In return they receive some companionship, arm candy for various business and social events and maybe even some sex when required. Yucch! The thought of that almost made me sick. Some old, fat guy on top of me.

I finally gave in and ended up saying I would go. Uncharacteristically for me I was already flustered by what I would wear.

Let's be honest here, I had never really cared about what I wore! I was confused as to why the heck I even cared now, but I still spent that night searching through my closet. Perhaps this was part of being normal? Wanting to just fit in.

I knew I was reasonably attractive, and I was very confident in my skills and abilities. Thanks to a Mexican father who was always in amazing physical shape and a beautiful and powerful mother from Boston I was blessed with the right genetics. I got my father's sense of survival and his athleticism along with my mother's intelligence and ability to sniff out facts. On top of that the mix of a somewhat aristocratic white woman with a very handsome Mexican man gave me unique looks. During my career that had helped me a great deal. Now that I was trying to be a regular citizen, I found it often hurt rather than helped me.

A lot of my confidence, however, came about because of what I had done. I wished so often that I could share some of the details of my career the way other people can. Unfortunately, Special Ops training and my job did not necessarily translate to regular life and regular conversations. It was not like hanging around with the guys and chatting about the last mission. That was the thing I missed most about doing what I had been doing before. We each knew exactly what the dangers were and what the possible outcomes could be. As such, you had a camaraderie that one could not get anywhere else. I knew I would have to work hard at it so that I wasn't discovered.

Being about five-feet-nine and 146 pounds of solid muscle, I had a lot of confidence on the athletic field, in the gym, almost in any sport or challenge. I could go head-to-head with just about anyone and if I wanted to win, I knew I could. Perhaps because of, or maybe despite, this I found myself wishing I could just wear my training shorts and sports bra and show up like that. Better yet, all black clothes with a blacked-out face and carrying one or two concealed weapons. THAT was how I really liked to show up at a gathering!

I knew how I looked in that type of outfit. I felt confident and, generally speaking, it was the other people who were "scared" of me. I have powerful legs and upper body strength most women would not appreciate. My breasts were smaller and that was good with me as they didn't often get in the way. When I dressed up, I still looked like a woman and wasn't butch or anything, so I liked myself for the most part. In fact, both men and women had commented on my looks. Thanks again Mom and Dad.

I forced myself to look through my closet and ended up being thankful it was only Tuesday. I had plenty of time to hit the mall and do some shopping. The girls said it was a casual type thing and not to wear a dress or anything too dressy. We would be spending most of our time in the back yard. Kathy suggested I bring a bathing suit as there would most likely be swimming at some point. Oh geez, I had to find a bathing suit too! That was always a struggle for me.

People looked at me one way when I was fully clothed but completely differently when more of me was revealed. Men and women both would notice my power and strength.

The other issue with bathing suits was that I was carrying around a few battle wounds. I took to explaining away the two scars you could see as being birth defects. I was always hoping that there would not be a doctor in the group who would know what a surgically repaired deep knife wound or a bullet hole really looked like. I was sure that Los Angeles was crawling with plastic surgeons from what I had seen in the last two or so years, so it was a real concern for me.

I still have a tough time getting the knife wound situation out of my head. I could have easily been dead, except for my off-the-chart skills in self defense.

It was an operation in Chechnya where I was virtually alone in the whole country. There were a few safe places I could get to if needed but only two real escape routes. I either had to go around the Caspian Sea to Iran or below the Black Sea, over to Bulgaria and then to Greece. Neither would be an easy trip, but I would rather take the Black Sea route. I preferred to keep my tourist cover intact planning, if I got out, to head over to Greece for a bit. I would get in, see some sights, do my job and get the heck out. It was that very tourist cover that would cause a problem for me.

In my line of work there was always a chance one would get caught in a foreign country. If I was caught, I knew that as far as the USA went, they had no knowledge of me. I had a necklace that was always around my neck and tucked inside my shirt. I also had a cheap looking little belt I wore almost everywhere.

The only similarity between the two pieces was that each contained a small L-pill (lethal pill) cleverly hidden. Each pill contained a lethal dose of potassium cyanide that, when ingested, would cause death within minutes. There was no cure or way to revive someone who had ingested such a pill. Most who carried them realized it might be better to have a quick death rather than a long, drawn-out death-by-torture.

Enough about scars, back to my story.

I had completed my mission and the target was taken out with no fanfare. I was confident that when the body was discovered it would be determined he broke his neck after a risky dive off the jagged cliffs. I knew where the man liked to swim and that he occasionally jumped off those cliffs. The locals knew this as well. If he were to have, let's say, a diving accident that would not be out of character. It was highly unlikely, if it were properly executed, the authorities would think anything was suspicious.

I must have swum in that water for hours, four days in a row until finally my opportunity presented itself. There were no other people around and my target showed up. I saw him swimming and I noticed that both sides of the cliffs and the water were out of anyone's sight. I scampered up the cliff and prepared to dive in.

I dove in close to him and as I came up, swam up behind him and with one twist snapped his neck. I pulled him over to a shallow part of the water and rammed his head against a submerged rock. I ensured the wound would support the angle of the break on his neck and I swam away. I was confident the local medical authorities would never rule this anything but an accidental death. There were always accidents where some bozo tried to dive off a cliff and struck shallow rocks. They would have no reason to think anything different in this case.

I escaped without being discovered and made my way over to Greece. My mistake, one I never made again, was letting my guard down once I was safely in Greece. I decided after getting out of Chechnya successfully, that I could allow myself a few days to disappear. I planned to head to a place I had been to a few times, Mykonos.

One of the perks of my job was that I travelled to many different places and sometimes I was able to extend the trip like this.

Sure, I was typically there to assassinate someone, but I still got to see many of the sights! It was fun to be just another tourist although I always had to be vigilant. In this case, I had taken out the target and had no reason to believe I was followed, or anyone knew who I was. I just wanted to relax.

I knew the casino in Mykonos was a fun place to hang and there were some great swimming spots too. The weather was perfect for a little R&R. I was having a great couple of days and even met a handsome Greek man to spend a little time with. He was a lot of fun and a welcomed distraction. I suppose I should have realized that, with those guys, keeping things platonic was highly unlikely. They moved quickly, and this one was no different.

We were out at the casino, and he suggested a drink and a walk on the beach. I hadn't had any normal male companionship for a long time, so I didn't see any harm in hanging with him. We had strolled for quite a while when I noticed we were now on a deserted section of beach. He was next to me, and I sensed, perhaps even saw, the movement. He was coming at me, with a knife in his hand and mumbling something in Russian. Crap! How could I be so stupid? Fortunately, I had not completely lowered my guard. I slipped the blow and knocked the knife out of his hand.

I had confidence now as there are few people on the planet whom I cannot defeat in hand-to-hand combat. I instantly searched the ground for a potential weapon but saw nothing, other than sand. I dug my feet in and braced myself, so I could generate power.

I struck him hard enough for him to realize he was in a real scrap, so he stepped up his game. We exchanged blows at close quarters with him catching me with a hard shot to my ear that staggered me. I saw stars briefly as I fell backward onto the sand. He came at me, and I threw sand up into his eyes. The problem was he had recovered the knife and sliced me pretty good on the side of my body. I allowed him to think I was seriously hurt but I was ready for him to come in for the kill.

He did just as I expected, and I adjusted my position slightly, so I could trap his arm on the way in. A quick twist of the hands and his full bodyweight drove him down onto his own blade. I pushed and twisted further up into his ribcage, and he was dead in seconds as the blood gushed from his heart. I got up and brushed myself off. I confirmed he was dead and quickly left the area after extracting the knife from his chest.

I stopped to wrap myself up tightly to slow the bleeding and washed off in the water. It was important to keep the seawater out of my wound as the oceans are teeming with bacteria. I cleaned any prints off the knife and tossed it as far as I could into the ocean.

It would likely sink out of sight never to be found and would rust away over time. Getting rid of evidence was second nature to me.

I now had a deep gash that I needed to have fixed without going near a local hospital. Luckily, I knew some places where I would be safe and could get patched up. I moved cautiously through the city toward my destination, hoping the contact person was still the same. I was able to have my wound repaired by a local doctor the agency had and I got out of there as soon as I could.

And now here I was in Southern California just trying to live the life of a gym-rat, beach person who liked to surf. It really is a wonderful place to live. Beaches everywhere, a million things to keep oneself busy and year-round great weather. I really loved Southern California. I really don't think I will ever want to live anywhere else.

That was one of the great stories I could tell at a party if I was ever able to divulge anything about my past. I quickly got back to the party preparations. Fortunately, I had nothing but time on my hands. I planned to head to the mall the next day to check out my favorite stores. I was most comfortable on my Harley, but I didn't want to ride that over. That also meant my usual wardrobe choices, jeans, T shirt and riding boots, were out the window.

I approached the mall with a certain amount of trepidation but decided the best approach would be to hit a couple of stores and let the staff do their job. I went to at least six stores and fortunately found two that had seemingly good managers, both of whom were close to my size and shape. I was confident that would work best, so I went to each, told them about the party and the casual dress requirement and asked them to help me select outfits. I truthfully said I just had no skill in this department and really needed help.

They were both quite good, but I ended up spending the most time at one store as I just clicked better with that lady. She was about the same height and weight as me and she understood my athletic build. As we started to look at clothes, she mentioned that it can be challenging for "girls like us" to make the right fashion choices.

I wholeheartedly agreed, and we had a little chuckle about sporty butts versus the currently in vogue big butts and then a few more laughs about breasts and guys. This lady got me, and I was confident we would find the right combination.

I left the store feeling quite happy with myself and thanked her profusely for all the help and time she spent with me. I had two outfits in my bag, the most likely one being a pair of dressy, although on the short side, shorts and a two-top combination.

The shorts really accentuated my legs and butt without being at all sleazy or revealing. The two-top combo would let me be comfortable without a bra and that was always a big win for me.

I didn't want anyone staring at my chest and I wanted to be as comfortable and cool as possible. I really didn't need to wear those things anyway. Besides, it's not like I was going to be running around or anything.

Now it was time to find a bathing suit and I initially thought that was going to be much more difficult. As I walked into the store and said hello the girl asked if I needed help. I said I did, and she immediately said, "I have the perfect suit for you." I almost walked out right then. I hated that crap but decided I should have a look anyway. This was a swimsuit specific store and the only one like it in the mall.

She accurately guessed my size and brought me a couple of suits, one a light purple and one black. I went into the change room as she followed close behind and waited by the mirrors. She said I would be the first to try these on, they were brand new styles.

She was mumbling about an athletic fit, but I had already tuned her out by that point. I tried on the black one first and damned if she wasn't right.

I stepped out into the hallway, and she said wow as I was trying to see all the angles in the mirrors. I will admit she called the fit perfectly.

The bottoms were kind of like a boy short, almost a shorter version of my favorite workout shorts. They showed my power and strength but also made me look lady-like too. The top was sort of a halter style with a hole in the middle to show a little bit of cleavage. It fully covered me but also showed that I had some curves up top. I decided that I liked it.

I told her the black one seemed a bit too much though. She said it looked perfect with my short black hair. I kept my hair as short as I always had, shorter than most men nowadays! I just always felt comfortable that way and did not want to give a target any edge so long hair was out. She told me the light purple one was the same style, why don't I try that one?

I did, stepped out and immediately decided that was the one. I thanked her, paid the bill and was on my way. I was quite surprised the whole thing was so easy, I was done by noon.

Maybe this whole civilian lifestyle could work for me after all. As I headed back to my car, I realized I had not had any sort of personal "maintenance" done for quite a while. There was no way I was planning to hook up with anyone, but I also liked to feel like I was always well kept. I may have been a killer in my previous life, but I wasn't a Neanderthal.

I made an esthetics appointment for the next day and went home. This was about the only time I did not feel the equal of any man.

They could get away with doing nothing to themselves, hair growing everywhere it could get a foothold and they were fine with it.

I went to the shop in the morning and told the lady I wanted "the works". She asked if I had a big date and I laughed and said not likely, I just hadn't had the full meal deal for a few months now. She got started. I realized I really hated this stuff, but you had to do it.

Manicure, pedicure, waxing, it was an ordeal to be sure. Kathy and Angie were always asking me to go with them, but I just didn't see the attraction. To be honest, I would rather go through a couple of hours of full contact training rather than this type of thing any day. Sometimes I wondered why I wasn't born a man. So much less to take care of, so much easier to find clothes and the world was their bathroom if all they had to do was pee. Sometimes guys really pissed me off.

Once I was done though I will admit I felt rather good. I was ready for the party and a little socializing. At least as ready as I was ever going to be. I understood I couldn't remain a hermit forever at my age but too much social interaction tended to put me on edge.

I'm not sure if it was my version of PTSD but I was so used to knowing everything about everyone that when I did not it made me uneasy.

I was not as jumpy as I had been, but you still did not want to be the person who came up behind me and grabbed me by surprise. I had to work hard to keep my reactions in check.

Chapter Three – Party Night

Saturday arrived, and I headed over to Kathy's house. It was a start in the afternoon kind of thing, so I was dressed appropriately. The shorts and two top idea was casual, and I didn't look like a slob. Overall, I felt surprisingly good. I took a cab over to her house as there was no way I would have chanced driving impaired when this shindig was over. I brought a small bag with me to carry my suit and a few other things. I had a coverup in there and a sweater too just in case. Southern California was typically nice, but it also cools down at night every now and then, so I wanted to be prepared. The ocean breezes tended to cool things down quickly once the sun disappeared.

The driver let me out and I walked up to the large ornate front doors of what looked like quite a spacious home. It seemed we were close to the beach but as I wasn't driving, I really had no idea how far away it was. I knocked, Kathy opened the door, gave me a big hug and brought me inside. I was floored by the house, even just standing in the foyer. This place was a little more than "quite" large. It was massive. Then I noticed you could see right through it to the ocean out the back! Their back "yard" was the freaking Pacific Ocean. I should have figured they would have beach front property.

It was a contemporary home with its own almost-private section of beach!

We walked through to the back, and I saw there were large trees lining each side of their whole yard, right to the edge of the sand. The whole lower level was windows or doors, and it was now completely open to the large party-patio. It was spectacular, even by California standards. There was a long, narrow pool that pointed out towards the gleaming blue waters of the Pacific. I had never seen anything like this and found myself saying holy cow at every stop of the tour. If I lived here, I don't think I would be able to find a good reason to ever go out.

Kathy said I was the first one there and she took me down to the lower-level patio to meet Jonathon. There were stairs off the end of the pool patio that took us closer to the sand and another patio below that. I heard a hello as we descended the steps and was somewhat shocked to see a tall, attractive, young man working away to get things ready.

Kathy took me over and introduced me. Jonathon took my extended hand and kissed it. I hadn't seen that done in a while and thought it was a little corny! He looked at me, smiling a 1,000 watt smile full of perfect teeth and said, "bet you thought I was an old bald guy, didn't you?"

I felt like I was about to blush, which I never did, but burst out laughing instead. He shook my hand this time, said he was pleased to meet me finally and said he loved my laugh. Odd, I always thought my laugh was a little too gruff, one of the least lady-like things about me.

I think it was an adaptation to my previous employment where "giggling" or laughing demurely was not something I would ever want to do.

Just then the bell rang. Kathy excused herself, telling us to get to know each other. I have to say I was taken with his looks and as he was just wearing some board shorts, I was also impressed with the shape he was in. He had a nice tan that made his rippled abs look even better. He was quite tall, and his eyes glinted as he smiled. Kathy had been coy about this guy for sure. They looked like your basic gorgeous, wealthy California couple. She a hot beach bod, bikini-wearing cute blond and he the picture of health club fitness combined with boyish charm.

Just then I heard a loud "hey there" and I turned to see Angela and her husband Lucas. As they walked down the stairs one couldn't help but notice how attractive they both were too, another perfect California couple! I was starting to notice these people were everywhere.

I had never met Lucas before either but knew his name. As he approached and extended his hand I said, "you must be Lucas." He smiled broadly, said I looked exactly like a "Meg" should and told me his friends called him Luke. He had some sort of accent, maybe Spanish or something and what could best be described as swarthy good looks. He looked like that actor-guy, Adam Rodriguez only a little more refined. Or perhaps a young Antonio Banderas. You get the idea. He was no mutt, that's for sure.

I found out, during the day, that Luke was from Brazil. I thought I could listen to his voice all day long. He spoke with an eloquence that made him seem like an actor or something. Sort of like a British guy but with more of a smoldering sexy tone. He wasn't an actor, but I thought he easily could be. Turns out he was some sort of financial analyst guy and he and Jonathon worked for a large company in that space. I was later to find out these two owned the company.

That certainly explained how Jonathon could afford what I was sure was at least a ten-million-dollar oceanfront mansion. I would find out later that Luke lived just up the beach in a similar shack. No wonder Kathy and Angela could spend their days going to lunch, shopping and the gym.

People started to arrive in groups and suddenly it seemed the house, patio and beach were full. Luke and a couple of other guys had grabbed surfboards and were out trying to catch some waves. I watched Luke as he stepped out of the changerooms, and he looked like a male model too. He had a tan that darkened his already dark skin a little more. He was in at least as good a shape as Jonathon was, with another set of obviously rock-hard abs. He had broad shoulders and powerful arms that tapered down to a narrow waist. Both had muscular thighs, so I knew they trained in the gym regularly. You didn't get quads like theirs without serious weight room time.

I thought both these guys looked like they could give me a run for my money in a fight, but I quickly decided they were more pretty-boys than functional. That was obviously fine for Kathy and Angela but any man who would be with me would have to be close to my equal. I didn't figure there were many of those around, so I really wasn't looking too hard.

I also think I am more of an acquired taste. I was always drawn more to the forceful bad-boy type anyway. I suppose that was a function of where I had worked and with whom I had worked in the past. It likely had something to do with my father as well.

I always found that type of guy was a better fit for me, it was almost like a buddy thing. I didn't particularly enjoy things like Opera, or the Ballet so refined men were not my type. When it came to orchestras my favorites would be Guns N Roses, Led Zeppelin or even Justin Timberlake, anything but the LA Philharmonic.

The day wore on and after a bit the girls said they were putting on their suits and hitting the pool. Their pool had a totally cool swim up bar that was like a reverse island. It is a smaller version of the bars you saw in the pools at the big resorts in Cabo and elsewhere. They had even paid a bartender to tend bar for the party. This was getter better and better.

I went in to change with them and get into that pool. We were all just changing in the one room, no biggie as we did it all the time at the gym. Both girls were saying how they wished they could look like me and admiring how powerful I looked. I returned the compliment saying I wished I looked a little more girly sometimes, curvier and more bikini-like as they were.

I really didn't think that at all, but I figured it was a good thing to say. When they saw my new suit, they both said wow. They said it made me look like a million bucks. I laughed and said not as million bucks as your two old bald guys! We all had a good laugh about that. They said they wanted to tell me the truth before the party but decided to keep it a secret. They could tell I thought they had hooked up with a couple of old rich guys and wanted to see the look on my face when I met Luke and Jonathon.

They knew how hot their husbands were and found it humorous that I had jumped to the assumption they were mere trophy wives. To the contrary, both owned successful businesses but had been shrewd enough to find top-flight management to run them. They were only at work about once every two weeks and that was the limit of their job.

We were still chuckling as we left the room. As we came out of the change room a guy was stepping off the last step onto the patio.

He whistled and said how great we all looked. He told Kathy and Angela they looked awesome as always and then asked them to introduce him to the vision they were with.

Really, I thought? A vision? You've got to be kidding. I was never a fan of smooth-talking douchebags. He turned to shake my hand and said his name was Bobby as Kathy said, "this is Meg." He said how pleased he was to meet me and then took off saying he hoped we could have a drink later and chat a bit. I was kind of glad he didn't stick around.

I told the girls I thought he was a bit creepy. That was when they came clean and said they had told him about me and even showed him a photo. I pointed out that turnabout would have been fair-play and I would have liked some warning. Bobby was the number three person in their company, and they said he was just a little nervous. They told me a what a great guy he was, he had just never found the right woman.

I gave them both supreme heck and said they should have told me but in minutes it was all forgotten. We hit the pool and relaxed in the water while bartender Carlos made us each a drink. There is something very relaxing about having a good-looking shirtless bartender serve you drinks as you sit on a comfy pool stool half submerged. I supposed it was a wee bit better than sitting on a wooden box in the hot desert having an almost-cold beer.

We swam a bit, had one more drink and then I decided I wanted to hit the waves. I was a decent surfer and just felt like being away from the crowd for a while. There was never a bad day on a surfboard as far as I was concerned. Thanks to my previous line of work, I was still uncomfortable when I didn't have background information on everyone around me. I felt safer getting away for a bit and thinking, assessing things.

That always helped me to center myself and try to get back to living my new life. I asked Kathy if she had a medium length board I might like. She pointed one out, I grabbed it and headed into the waves. The waves were never too big this time of day so there would be no crazy rides, but it was always good to get out there on the ocean.

I paddled slowly out over the breaks, even having to dive under a couple of larger waves. Hmm, perhaps I would get in a good ride or two. I waited with the guys until I saw the third wave of a set coming in and began paddling hard. I jumped up on my board and had a decent first ride. I was still getting used to the board, but it was quite close to my own in size and shape, so I had a few good cutbacks and turned out before I got swamped.

As I crested the wave, I heard someone say, "nice ride." I turned to see it was Bobby. I smiled, said "thanks" and kept paddling out. We were now paddling side by side.

I looked over as we guided our boards over the waves and said, "can you surf or am I going to have to pull your sorry butt out of the water in a couple of minutes and revive you?"

I decided it was cute when he flashed a smile and said, "perhaps I WILL crash just so you'll have to give me mouth to mouth." As I said, I wasn't looking for anyone, but on the other hand I had not been with anyone for more than a year. As I contemplated that, I realized I had better be careful deciding. I was wound a little tight at the moment and didn't want to do something I would regret later, or sooner. There was a time or two when I had not made the best choice in this area of my life.

It struck me as odd because I was so skilled at profiling, reading people and evaluating situations and yet when my own heart was involved things somehow got muddled. I decided I needed to focus more during the initial stages of meeting someone new and keep my guard up.

Turns out Bobby was a stud surfer. He grabbed the next wave ahead of me and I watched as he cut back numerous times. I kept seeing him crest onto the top of the wave expecting him to crash hard any moment. He looked close and then would disappear down the face only to reappear at the top in a few more seconds.

Like my ride, he turned out on the last one and splashed back down over the crest smoothly, paddling quickly to get back out. Hmm, at least I might have a male friend to pal around with and surf together if nothing else.

We all caught a last wave in, dried off and changed and the party went on. It ended up being a lot of fun. I met more new people whose names I will never recall but generally had a good time. As the party wore down, I told Kathy and Angie I was taking off. They called me a cab and the four of them saw me off at the front door.

I went home alone after the party and slept well. I thought about Bobby a bit as I laid in my bed trying to get to sleep. It was nice to find a guy I could surf with, and he seemed much better than my first impression. Perhaps he really was just nervous as the girls had mentioned? I decided I would be open to whatever presented itself and see where it went. He was a good-looking guy and was a great surf partner too. In general, he was just fun like Jonathon and Luke.

We started to see each other more and more, usually at Jonathon and Kathy's. They had a lot of gatherings and parties, and they were always fun to be around. Money may not buy actual happiness, but it sure seemed to make it easier to BE happy.

They obviously had serious money and they were very happy people. Going to their place was always like one of those all-inclusive vacations. All the food and booze you could ever want and not a dime to be paid.

They would never think of allowing someone to bring their own booze or anything else to their parties. I tried a few times and was laughed at the first time and chastised the second. I eventually decided it was just easier to accept their hospitality.

Chapter Four - Dating

I had not envisioned myself dating anyone in quite a long while, but I was enjoying the thought of it. I had been out a few times with Kathy, Angela, their beaus and Bobby and we were all having a grand old time. A little bit like the old group date thing in high school but I was cool with that. It made it seem more like fun than anything that would get serious so that helped keep it all casual.

It was only a month after that party when the six of us were back at Jon and Kathy's partying and having fun. Bobby was sitting on the patio as I stepped out of the change room just a little self-conscious. I had purchased a new black bikini and, to be honest, I felt a little over exposed. I never wore a real bikini and always favored the longer board shorts with a full coverage halter style top. This was definitely not one of those. There was really very little left to the imagination and what was left was covered by the tiniest and thinnest of fabrics. I felt more like I was wearing lingerie that should remain hidden rather than a bathing suit to be worn in public.

Bobby looked up and just said, "wow, you look amazing." I smiled and said, "so do you sailor" and out we went. We spent a good chunk of the day on surfboards and paddleboards having a great time, all six of us. The water was a comfortable temperature, and the waves were just the right size.

Bobby was in as good a shape as the other two and I enjoyed watching him work a wave. Cutting back and trying to get inside even the smallest tube. He could really handle a board. He had been surfing for most of his life.

After a couple of hours of surfing, we went in to shore to change and hang on the patio while Jonathon cooked for us. He was quite the amateur chef and I loved eating at their house for that very reason. Bobby and I had kissed a few times by now, hugged a bunch but had not progressed too far past that point.

The reason I bought this bathing suit was that I had decided it was time. I needed release and I needed it to be at the hand of someone other than myself! I wasn't positive how I felt about Bobby yet, but it appeared he might be what I needed, so I figured why not? If you can't find Mr. Right then Mr. Right Now was always a close second.

As the day came close to an end, Kathy said there were spare rooms on the middle floor. We had all spent a good deal of time at the swim up bar and nobody was feeling any pain. Jonathon looked at us and said no way either one of you are driving, you're both staying here tonight.

Kathy and Jonathon took Angela and Luke to the third floor where there was a master and a guest room.

They pointed Bobby and me to the two rooms on the middle floor, warning us it was a jack-and-jill bathroom, so we needed to watch the door locks.

As we walked towards our respective rooms we kissed and said good night. He made no move to come to my room and I decided I was going to have to drive this. I was already under the covers when the bathroom door opened slightly, and Bobby told me he was just going to have a quick shower. I said good night but then noticed I did not hear the door lock.

I laid there as I waited to hear the water running and him in the shower.

I turned off my light, got undressed, waited a minute or two and decided I was going in. I moved quietly into the washroom and toward the shower.

The shower was a large one, all tile and stone and didn't have a door, curtain or anything. The glass block walls sort of overlapped each other so that you walked between them. I could see two large showerheads on the ceiling, one pouring water and the other off. I got next to the gap in the front shower wall and quietly asked if I could join him. I smiled as he said, "I thought you'd never ask". He turned on the other shower head to warm it up for me. Great shower etiquette I thought.

I stepped around the corner and underneath the water as Bobby drew in a breath and said, "my gawd, you ARE absolutely gorgeous." I pulled out my, "you don't look too bad yourself line" and moved towards him to kiss. In no time we were a flurry of hands and lips everywhere.

I can tell you one thing, when we exited that shower, we were cleaner than two people had ever been. There were suds and soap all over the walls and even the ceiling. It was a wild shower.

He took my hand and led me to his room where the festivities went on all night. He was a tremendous lover, taking care of all my needs. He was powerful, sexy and tender all at the same time. I decided we were a good fit even though he was not my usual type. In no circles would Bobby be considered a bad boy. Just the same, it was a stellar evening and I lost track of how many times he satisfied me.

My last recollection was dozing off in his arms. I awoke completely rested to have a shower before breakfast. I stepped into the shower and let the hot water cascade over my head and face as I stood underneath the rain head. I wasn't surprised when I felt arms embrace me from behind and hold me tight.

I said there was nothing happening this morning, I was worn out. His response was to fondle me and tell me I had the most beautiful butt he had ever seen. He spun me around, looked me up and down and said, "Who am I kidding, you have the most beautiful everything I have ever seen." We kissed briefly but I managed to escape. I was in no rush to do the whole relationship thing and did not want him thinking I was.

By the time I came downstairs Bobby was already at the table with everyone else. The whole back of the house was again wide open, and the cool, salty ocean breeze made the house smell amazing. Sunlight poured into the room washing over everything with a golden hue and made it so inviting. I sat down, and Jonathon poured me a coffee. We were all talking about how much fun yesterday was when Kathy finally blurted out how glad she was that something finally happened with me and Bobby. I blushed a little and asked what she was talking about?

Everyone laughed and said even though the walls were thick they heard exactly how much fun I was having. Kathy added that based on the "oh my gawd's", they also knew exactly how many times I had fun too. I hadn't realized that we were being too loud but then after more than a year I suppose that was to be expected. I had not been with too many men for a woman my age, but I was well capable of having a good time and providing directions to someone new.

I started laughing almost uncontrollably and looked at Bobby smiling and said, "the noise was all your fault big fella." He just grinned back at me and that was when it started for us.

Chapter Five – Getting Serious

Bobby and I saw each other a lot more after that night and were soon very exclusive. Funny enough he had a home not too far up the beach too, so I guess he was ready when I first jumped him. He could have easily walked home that night! When I confronted him with that fact, he told me he was just trying to play it cool and let me move at my own speed. He admitted he wanted me the first time he saw me. I decided he had made an excellent choice and we gradually got closer over time.

We got more serious and although I had no plans to marry him, or anyone else, I did agree to move into his beach house. I will admit that I did quite enjoy the whole oceanfront living aspect of it. We led an idyllic life for a short while. He didn't work too much but still left me enough alone time to hang with the girls and train the way I liked. Things were good. We surfed together and always had a fun time. We had quite a few dinner parties and lots of times there were clients invited too. Seemed like the three boys shared the whole keep the big clients entertained duties.

It was all rolling along nicely until one party. There were lots of people and Bobby had even hired servers and a bartender to handle all the hosting details. That way we could just entertain guests. The day was playing out well and everyone was having an enjoyable time. I was introduced to a couple and Bobby mentioned what a great surfer I was.

The guy grabbed my arm said, "let's go catch some waves" and off we went. I smiled and waved as we grabbed a couple of boards and spent the next two hours out on the water.

The waves were ideal that afternoon, perfect to surf all day with very little chance of any big crashes. Gentle four and five footers rolled in set after set. You would finish one ride and barely get paddled out when it was time to hop up again. He was a good surfer too and we were competing for the best waves in no time.

Surfing was one of the feelings I enjoyed the most. You watch for the right wave, paddle your butt off and then jump up onto your board. It is a whole different perspective when you're standing on that board and sliding, feeling weightless, down the face of a wave. Each time you dig in and cutback you get the same rush of falling down the face of that wave all over again.

I often thought that I could just surf all day, every day if there were enough waves. It was a Zen-like thing. I rode the last wave in, and we walked back up to the house. A few people commented on our surfing skills, which was nice to hear from a group of surfers. Like anything else, once I started it, I was committed to becoming the best I could be.

Later, after everyone cleared out, Bobby asked me what the hell I was doing out there. I said, "what are you talking about" and turned to walk away. He grabbed my arm forcefully and my first instinct was to spin and drop him. Had it been any other male he would be on the floor wondering what had hit him. But this was Bobby. I was confused. I didn't want my past uncovered though, so I just twisted my arm away.

I knew despite his physical strength and the shape he was in I could easily injure him so it's not like I was at all worried. We ended up just going to sleep that night. I certainly didn't want him touching me after that display. Thankfully he was at least smart enough not to push the matter. I was glad of who I was and felt bad for the women who were not able to push back the way I could.

When I got up in the morning, he had already made a big breakfast and had my coffee ready. He apologized freely for being such a jerk going on to explain he had had way too much to drink. I brushed it off and we went on about our day. He explained he had never done anything like that before and promised he would never do anything like that again. I spent a great deal of time over the next week thinking about what happened. I hadn't done anything wrong so why was he so bent out of shape?

I can't put my finger on the exact time I decided I had to get out, but I do remember planning my escape.

Things had progressively gotten worse and rougher. I was probably in love with him and thought I could work through it, but I almost snapped one night when he actually slapped me. I was flabbergasted when I didn't hit him back and immediately realized I needed to leave. How stupid could he be to punch ME anyway?

I had no idea what I was doing and could not understand how this happened. Why wasn't I defending myself? Why would I let someone hit me for no good reason? I had never allowed anyone to hit me without hitting back, hard. Why didn't I do that now? What was wrong with me?

This was not who I was or how I handled my life. The following Monday, I had my stuff packed and loaded in my car and I was ready to go by the time he got home in the early afternoon. I did not want to just disappear, that usually never ends well. We sat down on the patio in the sun, and I told him we were finished. I did not want to live here any longer. I said I was leaving right away, and he just went crazy. He was off the rails nuts, screaming, yelling, and saying if he couldn't have me nobody could. His eyes were dark and soulless.

He grabbed a knife and came towards me. Before he knew what had hit him, he was disarmed, laying on the floor bleeding from the mouth, with my foot on his chest and a tight grip on his arm. As I twisted his thumb back against his hand, I told him I was leaving now, and he was not to follow me.

I said I had a gun with me (although I didn't, nor did I need one to handle the likes of him) and I was not the least bit afraid to use it. I added that it would be in his best interests to just leave me alone and not bother me after this day. We just need to go our separate ways, and nobody needs to know about any of this. I released him and walked quickly out of the house to my car.

I got home locked my door and alternated between being mad and sad, trying to figure out where it all went wrong. I wanted to understand how I ended up like too many other women. Subservient or scared to stand up for myself. Not willing to simply leave. It wasn't like I had a lot of skin in the game. We did not own a house together or have kids. We didn't even have a dog. I was as mobile as I was ever going to be. I wondered how women who had children ever had the guts and commitment to leave an abusive man.

I realized they had true inner strength and in some ways were even tougher than I was. I knew I could crush the life out of this clown had I wanted to and yet I still did not leave. I didn't even defend myself. I just took it. Worse yet I was trying to figure out what I had done, as if I MADE him hit me.

Why did women always assume that it was something we did? Why was it so difficult for us to think that he might be the one with the problem?

That was when it started for me. That was what put me on the path I would soon follow. I thought about how many other women I had seen in similar situations. Disrespected, emotionally abused, even hit. I knew I had to do something about it.

Chapter Six- Gotta Get Out

I was now completely moved back into my house. Bobby started to show up close to the gym when I was there. I would see his car outside my place every now and then. I would bump into him at the grocery store occasionally. There were hang-ups on the phone. All the usual stalker type behaviors. He was even banging on my door one night at three in the morning. I decided then and there that I had to get rid of this jerk.

Of course, I couldn't do it right away. The police were not an option, I didn't want anyone knowing about my past. Besides, too often when women call the police in this type of situation it only gets worse anyway. I wanted to continue to live my life anonymously if I could. I felt the best way to do that was to use my skills and training as I had when I was in the forces. I would treat him like any other high value target. He was of the lowest value of course, but I would not let that stop me. I would eliminate him the same way I took out all the other creeps I had killed during my career. I would do my best to view him from a detached and analytical point of view from now on. As of this day, he was just another target, one more mission to complete.

I sat at my table and formulated a plan. I knew I needed to get away for a while first.

I would take my bike and go touring, visiting places I had always wanted to see but had not been to yet. I would make the break-up sound as normal and friendly as possible and tell the girls

I just needed to go riding to get some perspective. I knew that the first person anyone looked at in a murder or even accidental death was always the spouse or partner. People had seen that we were dating, and a couple even knew I had basically moved in. I also knew there were plenty of forensics available in his house to give me away. I needed to wait at least three months for all that to disappear naturally. Also, if I just went away there would be no stalking and he would likely find someone else to hook up with.

I did not feel good about turning him loose on another unsuspecting female, which would likely happen, but I had no choice. A nice clean break and a few months time should keep me out of the suspect pool when I did kill him. I knew I would eventually kill the creep, but I needed to put some time and space between me and him to keep myself off the radar. I met with the girls the next week and they were shocked to hear I was leaving for a while.

They asked what happened with Bobby and me and I told them it was all good, it was just time to go our separate ways. I didn't see how sharing the "he hit me" story would do any of us any good. It would also be something that could hurt me if I ever were considered a suspect.

I could not have anyone telling the authorities that I had been hit or abused in any way. That is the easiest way to move straight to the top of the suspect list.

Another week passed. Soon, I was loading up my bike with all my gear and heading out. I was looking forward to a nice leisurely ride through the Midwest, stopping whenever and wherever I wanted.

Sample some local beers, relax on some sunny patios and generally de-stress. There was nothing like a good motorcycle ride to clear the mind. Rumbling down the highways and backroads, sun on your face, as you leaned and accelerated through turn after turn. Sometimes it felt a little like slalom skiing when you were on the right road. On a warm day you could even get into a surfing mindsight on the right roads.

I saddled up early on a Tuesday and rode toward Phoenix, via Palm Springs. I loved riding through those mountains, it was always so relaxing. I enjoyed having nowhere in particular to go and no specific time to get there too. Sometimes it was simply good to put on some miles.

I put my feet up on the highway pegs, relaxed and cranked up the tunes so I could extract maximum enjoyment from this ride. I had Bob Seger's Roll Me Away blaring as I hit the highway...

> "Took a look down a Westbound Road, right away I made my choice. Headed out to my big two-wheeler I was tired of my own voice. Took a beat on the Northern Plains and just rolled that power on."

> "Twelve hours out of Makinaw City stopped in a bar to have a brew. Met a girl, we had a few drinks, and I told her what I decided to do. She looked out the window a long, long moment then she looked into my eyes. She didn't have to say a thing. I knew what she was thinkin...."

"Roll, Roll me away I want you to roll me away tonight. I too am lost; I feel double-crossed and I'm sick of what's wrong and what's right.

We never even said a word, we just walked out and got on that bike, and we rolled, we rolled clean out of sight. "

"We rolled across the high plains, deep into the mountains. It felt so good to me, finally feelin' free. Somewhere along the high road, air began to turn cold. She said she missed her home, I headed on alone."

"Stood alone on a mountaintop, starin out at the great divide. I could go East I could go West; it was all up to me to decide. Just then I saw a young hawk flying and my soul began to rise. And pretty soon, my heart was singing"

"Roll, Roll me away I want you to roll me away tonight. Gotta keep rollin, gotta keep ridin, keep searchin til I find what's right.

And as the sunset faded, I spoke to the famous first starlight I said next time, next time we'll get it right."

Bob Seger

Thanks Bob, to this day, it is still one of my most favorite songs. I start every long ride with that one blasting.

Chapter Seven – The Trip Starts

I made Palm Springs in no time and decided I needed to relax on a patio with a tasty, cool date shake. I loved date shakes! It was one my favorite things about that area. I sat there and fiddled around with my GPS and a map as I sipped my frosty treat, trying to find some fun routes to take. I knew there were some good ones to avoid the freeway as well as stay out of the sandiest part of that desert. Sand generally wasn't so good for motorcycles, and it was a little rough on the face too.

I finished my shake, mounted the GPS back on my bike and took off, headed out into a new adventure. The riding was smooth and enjoyable. There were nowhere near enough turns and curves on this section, but I could live with a straight road every now and then. I was likely an hour outside of Phoenix when I needed a bio-break, so I pulled off into a small rest stop below the road. There was only one other car there. I parked next to it and went to the women's side of the building.

I was washing my hands when I heard yelling outside. I dried my hands quickly and went out to make sure my bike was okay. Just as I rounded the corner, I saw this big Mexican dude punch his wife, or girlfriend, hard. I could tell she was out before she even hit the ground. Luckily, she fell back onto the grass and not the concrete.

To be honest, I couldn't believe what I was seeing. Something inside me snapped and I walked over to the jerk and started yelling at him.

He was a mountain of a man with a huge beer gut hanging over the belt of his dirty, oil-stained jeans. He started moving toward me telling me to mind my own damn business. I could see his right fist clenching and I prepared myself in case he took a swing at me. He had no idea who he was about to challenge. I was hoping he did a start a fight because I knew I would be the one finishing it.

He swung a huge meaty fist at me, and I just saw red as I easily dodged the punch. He was too big and far too slow to ever connect with that effort. I hit him full force in the middle of his chest. He staggered back but when he got his bearings, he came at me again and my instincts took over. I took him down by the arm and quickly hit him three times in the head, the last blow hard up into his nose.

That punch was often the coup de grace and unfortunately it got the job done this time too. I had not intended to kill the clown, I just wanted him to know that he should never hit a woman. There was blood everywhere, a dead Mexican at my feet and a still out-cold woman behind me. At least I knew she had not seen me yet and I decided there was only one way out. I could not wait for the police. No matter what had happened, it's always difficult to talk your way out of something when the other guy is dead.

I also knew I could never prove that I thought my life was in danger. My background and training would show that to be a blatant lie. I was highly trained by the US government in all methods of hand-to-hand combat, self defense and more aggressive solutions.

My training and experience would eliminate the need to use deadly force because my life could never be in danger from a guy like this. Heck, he could have been pointing a gun at me and the outcome likely would have been no different. I was certain if I stayed to explain I would be off to jail as soon as my background became known.

I knew I did not like being incarcerated. While I was still in training in the regular forces, I had spent just one long weekend in the brig after a little dustup. It was really nothing that warranted me being locked up, but I think the army was trying to send a message. You know, we're all equals here and that sort of thing. Apparently, they were already aware of my skills and talents and probably wanted to ensure I was a "company man".

I drug the greasy slob over to the edge of the road and pushed him down towards the river. I was hoping his obese body would roll right into the water like a big exercise ball. Unfortunately, he rolled deep into the bushes and stopped there. I did not have time to go down and try to get him into the water. I had to leave before the woman came to.

I was able to get on my bike and get out of there. I saw the woman get to her feet in my mirror just as I turned onto the highway. I was fairly sure I could not be identified but rode hard and fast for quite a while anyway. I needed to put miles between myself and that scene.

At that point I could not get to Phoenix soon enough. Along the way I decided I would rather push it and get to Tucson instead. I felt that would be a safer option. I didn't want to sleep too close to a place where I had just killed a man. I rode straight through Phoenix and continued down highway 10 Southeast to Tucson. That road is the definition of boring riding. I was kept alert trying to stay alive amongst all the poor drivers rumbling along oblivious to all around them at 80 and 90 mph.

As I approached Tucson there were several hotels on the outskirts, but I thought I would be better off being right in town, so I carried on. I knew there was a great restaurant there, so I plugged La Cocina into my GPS and when I got close, I began to look for a hotel nearby. I found a great motel where I could park my bike in a safe spot and walk to the restaurant. My bike would be hidden, and I had lots of options when it came time to leave just in case something happened. I really wasn't looking for trouble, but it seemed to be finding me quite easily.

I checked in at the front desk and got a ground level room close to my bike. I went in and washed the blood off my shirt in the sink, showered, changed and strolled over to the restaurant. I had a nice big margarita and was snacking on some chips and salsa when I spotted a newsflash on the TV. Luckily the sound was on, so I could listen as I watched them interview the lady who had been knocked out.

She was standing next to her car in tears as they spoke. Her face was a mess and even though she was clearly upset I knew that I had done the right thing. She would never have to worry about that jerk hitting her again.

She might be sad for a while but when she realized she could have easily been the dead one I was sure she would thank me if given the opportunity.

The news guy then walked over to the edge of the road and my heart sank as I knew what I was about to see.

I had hoped the light rain would have washed away any blood and they might miss the body. I suppose that was too much to hope for after doing something so impulsive. Sure enough, there were about four people down there working around that pig.

The news guy said he was dead, and they had no leads and local police were still digging for clues.

It would have been highway patrol jurisdiction, so I had no idea why he would say local police. The oddness of that statement put me on high alert. He could have just mis-stated that fact, but I thought it unlikely that was the case.

I was able to finish my meal and began a slow walk back to the hotel planning my next move. It was clear and warm, and the stars were out in full force. I always liked Tucson, for me it was exactly what Arizona was about. Warm air, comfortable evenings and adobe style homes everywhere.

I wished I could hang here for a few days, but I did not want to stay close. I just strolled leisurely back to my room taking in the night.

Chapter Eight – A New Plan

As I walked back to the motel I started to think, what was wrong with guys like Bobby and that Mexican? Why were they allowed to remain walking this earth? I flashed back to watching that pig knock out his wife and the feeling of satisfaction as I hit him once, twice and then that final fatal blow. I enjoyed the sensation of feeling his bones and his skull crack under my fist.

That was when it hit me, I missed the feeling of taking a bad life. I really could not remember how many lives I had ended but I figured no matter what the reason, I was on my way to hell now anyway. I might as well make it worthwhile. Today felt very worthwhile to me.

As I walked under the stars, I decided then and there I would take a few more jerks like that out before I turned my attention to Bobby. I could make it look like he was just another in a series which would throw suspicion away from me I hoped. I slept soundly that night, content in the knowledge my life would again have a higher purpose. Content that I was going to make the planet a safer place for many women.

As I awoke, my thoughts immediately turned to planning. I obviously did not want to get caught. Especially not before I got back to Bobby.

I had in depth knowledge of intelligence and forensics and was skilled in evidence identifying and gathering. That also made me skilled in evidence avoiding! I knew how profilers, local cops and national forces thought. I understood how they worked, how they worked together and how they did not work together. I had been well trained and extraordinarily successful avoiding everything from the SVR to the CIA to Mossad. I had even, for a brief period, been captured by the FSB, one of Russia's successors to the KGB. An extremely dangerous group of people is an understatement.

From here on I would plan a pattern that really wasn't a pattern. I would make it impossible for anyone to figure out where I had been or where I was going next. I was highly trained in counterterrorism, identifying terrorists and ferreting them out. I was top of the class in both forensic analysis as well as profiling. I knew this calling was the culmination and best use of everything I had been trained to do. The government had given me the perfect training to do exactly what I was now planning. Rid the earth of more bad guys and remain anonymous while I did it.

There were no little voices in my head or anything like that. I wasn't crazy. I just knew that I could do good by doing bad and that would make my life worth living. I could save innocent people while eliminating bad people, exactly what I had been so thoroughly trained to do. It just felt right.

Sadly, I also knew that to disguise my motive and reasons I might need to take the odd innocent life. I would do my best to find some not so innocent ones to lessen the guilt I knew I would feel. I knew that I would have to take a woman or two, so the pattern would not present itself to those who would soon be tracking me. I had never taken an innocent life and there was never collateral damage when I was working. I did not want to start now but it appeared I may not have a choice. I thought long and hard about that.

I decided on Albuquerque as my next destination. I loved the name of that place and had always wanted to see it so that's where I headed. Now that I had both purpose and plan the ride was good. Smooth, almost perfect roads snaking across a desert-like landscape. A little hot and dry to be sure but I was good with that. I had always fared quite well in a desert environment anyway.

Thanks to riding a big Harley, I could carry all the things I needed including nice cold water and some snacks in a cooler bag inside one of my saddlebags. Underneath that bag I would stash some of the tools I would need, being sure to buy things in multiple cities and towns along the way. I had a large stash of cash and would draw no attention to myself operating like this. Just another unobtrusive tourist picking up a couple of items.

I decided I would "help" a maximum of two women in and around any given city. Provided I disguised things by using different kill methods and wasn't spotted, I felt I could remain safe from detection. I knew I could operate in secrecy as I had done so in some of the most dangerous places on earth and come out unscathed. The more difficult part would be identifying targets and then isolating them, so I could complete my grisly task.

On the way to Albuquerque, I stopped in a couple of places to pick up the first of my tools. A skipping rope, some thick wire, a couple of corkscrews and some mechanics nitrile gloves. I would use the wooden handles from the skipping rope and the wire to create a garrotte, the corkscrews for my wine (or some bad guy's temple) and the gloves for obvious reasons.

It was always good to have multi-use items. Picking them up at larger stores along the way was a great method to avoid detection or accidentally revealing a travel pattern. Using cash was always a big help too. Using cash, subtle disguises and avoiding security cameras one could escape notice for years and operate unfettered. Some of the most famous serial killers known operated in a similar manner.

The keys were knowing what you were doing, commitment to detailed planning and using weapons that were readily available. Guns were the worst choice. Something like the garotte was a better choice provided you were skilled in fighting at close quarters and had the strength required. I possessed both qualities. I liked the garotte and always felt it was an under-rated weapon.

It was popular with the mafia in North America but had been used in many other countries for years. The beauty of it is that it is simple and untraceable. There are many ways to make one and the supplies to do so can be found almost anywhere. Such a weapon is untraceable.

All you needed was a couple of handles and some strong wire and you could make one in minutes. Cheap, effective and compact, it truly was an ideal disposable weapon. You merely had to get behind a person, make a loop of the wire by crossing your hands and then pull it tightly around the neck. It had the added benefit of preventing the target from screaming or making any noise when enough pressure was applied.Provided you had reasonable strength, it was also impossible to escape. Death usually came quickly and quietly.

I packed the supplies under my saddlebag and headed back out onto the highway. I approached the next town and had to laugh when I read the road sign. Truth or Consequences, 2 miles ahead. The irony was not lost on me. There would be no truth, only consequences for these dogs.

I stopped at a funky little restaurant called The Pacific Grill. I had an excellent seafood meal which I thought was odd with no water close-by.

I liked to have a lot of fish as it supported my training regimen that I was keeping up with while on the road. I had running gear with me, workout gloves and that was all I really needed. It would be good to find a sparring partner but that would be too dangerous. I could use plyometrics to help keep me battle-ready and you could do that just about anywhere.

I completed my meal and rode North toward Albuquerque arriving in the late afternoon and feeling motivated to start my "work". I got checked into a room, parked my bike safely out of the way and turned on the tube.

I had no idea how long it would take to acquire a target nor how long it would take to complete each mission, but I was in no rush. I saw the news come on and was horrified to see a picture of the Mexican again! I was in a whole different state, why the heck would that be on the news here? I turned the volume up a bit just in time to see a well-dressed guy calling himself Special Agent Sharpe talking about the crime scene.

He was explaining that the woman had seen a motorcycle pulling out and she remembered noticing it had a California plate. Those darn plates were too easy to recognize! I would have to fix that when I got a chance.

He said because this crossed state lines that the FBI, namely, Special Agent Colin Sharpe was now in charge.

There was nothing else disclosed, but I knew they always held a few things back. I began to wonder how much they really knew. He didn't scratch me or hit me at all so there was none of my DNA to be found. Out of habit, even though not wearing gloves, my prints would be nowhere either. You could really do quite a few things with feet and elbows rather then using your hands. I wasn't worried but recommitted myself to being super-careful.

I decided my first task was to register my bike here and get a New Mexico plate. It should be easy enough. I just needed to find an old couple whose name and address I could use. They never kept a close eye on their personal information, especially in the age of the internet. I had packed my ID kit with me, so I could quickly and easily create new and untraceable names complete with Driver's license and even passports if I needed one of those to complete the picture. I also had a few credit card blanks with me too, but cash was still the number one option.

I had to get out and pick up some clothes to help me disguise myself. I needed to look as average and unassuming as possible if I were to stay on track. I went and picked up some T shirts, a jean-jacket and some other jeans so I would blend in here. I even got a pair of work boots I worked hard to scruff up, so they didn't look so new. When I got the clothes, I also picked up a few camping-related items. Aluminum tent pegs, a wienie roasting stick and some other small items. I got a few pairs of deerskin gloves too, never knew when those might come in handy.

The tent peg was another ideal weapon that few people in my line of work considered using. Untraceable and no reason for anyone to think it was a weapon. Of course, once you killed someone with one you did not want to keep any others around. It was strictly a single use type method. They were light aluminum but structurally strong. Driving one deep into the ear canal of a person meant certain and speedy death. When faced with the need to kill someone at close quarters, the quieter the better. I found that I could kill someone this way while other people were sometimes only a few feet away and they would be none the wiser.

I went over to the senior centre the next day and hung around out front until I saw a likely target. I followed her to an older house, got the address and then waited for the mailman. I grabbed an envelope out of the box at the sidewalk and walked away. I now had a last name and address I could use.

I had everything I needed and went about creating an alias, used that address and got ready to go. I used the old couple's last name with a new first name to make myself a Driver's license. I then created an insurance form with that same information. All you really needed was that to register a vehicle. I also had an in-state bill of sale, so I wouldn't need an inspection or any other information. They made it so easy for people like me.

By the time I left, I had a New Mexico plate on my bike and a driver's license of a blond who looked nothing like me! She was forty pounds heavier than I, wore glasses and was fifteen years older.

There was no connection except height to the real me, but the boots with lifts inside helped to hide that too. I was now barely noticeable and certainly would not stand out anywhere I was going to be in this region.

There were lots of women around here with lineage like mine, so hiding in plain sight was easy.

Chapter Nine – Finally, My Next Target

I got back to the room and assembled my garrotte. A few tight wraps of the wire around each skipping rope handle, a secure knot and it was ready to go. I wrapped it into my jacket pocket along with both deerskin and the nitrile gloves and took off.

It was only a short walk over to what was clearly the seedy part of town and I found a bar right away. I took a seat at a small table in the corner and ordered a water and lime along with a beer. I had to keep my wits about me so no way I was going to have more than one drink. That being said, nothing beats a nice cold beer after riding. I just sat there and watched and waited while I nursed my beer and sipped on my water. I figured soon enough a target would identify himself.

It took a while, but as the night wore on, the place got hopping and things got louder. I sat and watched from under my baseball cap. Sure enough there was some noise across the bar, and I headed over that way to pretend to use the washroom. I walked by a table and heard some dirtbag yelling at his wife/girlfriend/whatever that she was a stupid slut. I looked at him and thought he had good potential, but we would have to wait and see. From here on I would make no mistakes. I would choose wisely and execute my plans as discreetly as possible.

I returned to my table keeping on eye on them and watched as he dragged her by the arm out of the bar. Luckily, they were walking so I was able to trail behind them at a safe distance. He berated her the whole way, and I was close enough, or he was loud enough, that I could hear him call her a fat bitch amongst other derogatory things.

I watched as he suddenly slapped her, and she fell onto the grass. I just about snapped right there but maintained my cool and watched them as they turned in to a ramshackle little house down a side street. I saw them walk up the crooked, grass infested sidewalk tripping all the way. The well-worn front door looked like it had been kicked in more than once.

I thought it was most likely local police responding to a domestic violence call. Even if that was not the case for all, it appeared to be a house typical for the area. It was run down, barely painted and small, likely with two bedrooms a kitchen and a front room.

I turned into the gravelled alley and found a small garden shed in their back yard. Conveniently, it had a window facing the house and the door was unlocked. I slipped in unnoticed by anyone and watched and waited. Sure enough, I saw them through the window. There was yelling and slapping and suddenly everything got quiet.

I continued to watch and saw a light go on in what I thought was the bedroom. I saw one more slap to her face and then nothing.

I decided I had to get a closer look. I snuck up to the window and peaked over the sill where I saw him on top of her. It was obvious what he was doing to her, and she was just as obviously, out cold. I could feel my blood boiling. I had to control my emotions better, calm down, and get back to being methodical and professional about what I was doing. I had to treat these like any other mission I had been assigned.

I could not leave her alone with him as I had no idea how this would end. I crouched low and moved toward the back door. I easily picked the cheap lock, stepped inside and moved silently down the hallway. I had my garotte in my left hand but as I went to move around the corner he was suddenly right in my face. Apparently, he was a minute-man, that figures. He reeked of liquor and cigarettes, and he was close enough I could smell his disgusting breath mixed with terrible body odor.

He tried to punch me, and my self defense training kicked in before technique could take over. He was dead on the floor from one well placed blow up into the bridge of his nose. Crap!

All that work to NOT create a pattern and all the planning to make each kill different and I had already screwed it up. I used the same blow, delivered by the same hand as the Mexican. That was not wise nor was it reflective of the training and efficiency that had been my calling card in my past life. I moved quietly out of the house and took the back streets, returning to my hotel. I had my disguise on but avoiding contact with anyone else was superior to even the best of disguises.

I got inside my room, calmed myself down and realized I had better improve the implementation of my plan or this would never work.

I needed to get back to the basics. I had to use all my skills and talents to ensure I could continue. I couldn't figure out why I was not my usual efficient and invisible self and remembered it had been almost three years since I had been on active duty.

Nothing keeps your skills sharper than KNOWING at any give time you are seconds away from being caught or killed. That knowledge, when used correctly, keeps you sharp. That knowledge keeps you alive.

I needed to get my edge back. I knew that the right activity would do just that. Sure, I had been training like a fiend but, much like sports, you can only practice so much. You had to play the game to truly improve. I viewed it as like coming back from an injury. I started slow, eased into it but in no time, I would hit my stride and be back at 100%.

Chapter Ten – Special Agent Colin Sharpe

I surveyed all the awards and citations on my office wall. I could remember at which point in my career each one was bestowed upon me. Agent Sharpe, Special Agent Sharpe and soon to be Supervising Special Agent Sharpe I had at one time hoped. All awards I had earned trying to be the best FBI agent I could be. Almost everyone here had their own self-love wall as we liked to call them. We had the market cornered on plaques, awards and photos with politicians and other famous people. I was always amazed how so public an organization could have so many agents who operated anonymously.

Of course, one wall was the famous FBI Most Wanted list. Our office kept a second wall of past most wanted's who had been caught. Each face with a large red circle and a line through it. Below that a plaque carrying the name of the senior agent who led the capture. I had my own name on three of those plaques on our wall, no small feat.

The FBI most wanted list was created by J. Edgar Hoover in 1950. There have been 518 fugitives on that list and as of today 484 have been caught or killed. California leads the pack with eighty-five people named.

The list itself reveals some remarkably interesting facts. The shortest stay on this list was Billy Austin Bryant in 1969. He lasted a whole two hours before he was captured. The longest by far was Victor

Gerena who was on the list for more than thirty-two (32) years! The last person added to this notorious list was Rafael Caro-Quintero.

Quintero is wanted for alleged involvement in the kidnapping and murder of a DEA agent along with connections to multiple drug trafficking organizations. At a solve rate of 484 out of 518, you did not want to show up on this list! The other key fact, and one of my favorites is that of the 518 people who have been on the most wanted list, only TEN were women.

As a fifteen-year FBI agent who graduated top of my class I was frequently assigned the most difficult cases, no matter where they were. In almost all situations, I closed those cases. I had an excellent close percentage by any standards. I failed to understand why a simple across-state-lines murder was now sitting on my desk.

I will admit that as I started to review the facts, I was slowly becoming more interested. Nevertheless, it seemed a long way below my experience level and pay grade. It looked like something more suitable for a junior agent to cut his or her teeth on.

There was precious little to go on except that the killer rode a motorcycle with California plates. I thought it would most likely be a Harley but who knows at this point? Not necessarily a bike gang, but that option would be in the mix. Oddly the only witness could not even tell me if it was a man or woman or provide any description at all really. In many cases, although eyewitnesses were notoriously unreliable, I found that details could also come out later.

As people moved further from the trauma their memories often produced new information, previously forgotten, or ignored. Due to the strength required and the precision of the killing blow I was biased towards it being a male, but I knew enough to keep an open mind. I had worked and trained with some female agents who could handle themselves against anyone. The dead fellow's wife really wasn't a font of information either. That was to be expected. In cases like this they were often conflicted with a sense of loss but also a sense of relief. The abuse would stop but now she had nobody to protect her from other dirtbags. We got our photos of the scene, interviewed the woman a couple of times and got the file started.

I questioned her and when I asked why they were stopped there when they lived close-by, she said she was feeling ill. I could see some slight bruising on her face under the makeup, even though it was only a day later. Further prodding revealed that he had hit her, and it had happened before. Many times before I would guess.

Of course, we always look at the spouse first in these cases, but I knew it was impossible for those flabby arms to deliver the blows that killed that guy. It was even less likely she would have been able to make the single strike that killed him. If he would have been shot or stabbed, then maybe she would have warranted a closer look. Had he have been poisoned she would have been my number one suspect.

She was quickly eliminated as a possibility, and I directed the lab to get me all the forensics as soon as humanly possible. There wasn't much. A tire tread from a motorcycle in the dirt and that was about it. Motorcycles all had pretty much the same tires so that would be of little use but of course the molds were locked away with whatever other meagre evidence there was. There was the off chance it might be a motorcycle specific tire though and anything would be helpful. I was successful because I never overlooked even the tiniest detail or anomaly.

I figured this was headed nowhere but I had our people contact surrounding police departments and ask them to keep their eyes peeled for any odd deaths. I knew details would eventually catch this person and I did not like to lose! Each department was left with my contact information and instructions to share with me immediately anything they found. I really didn't expect much but it was standard procedure.

I was shocked when two days later we received a transmission from the Albuquerque PD. A woman had awoken in the morning to find her husband dead on the floor. There was a pool of blood around his head and officers were on scene. After a few more questions it sounded like there could be a connection. I asked them to please lock down the scene for me and I was on a jet within twenty minutes. They were kind enough to have a car meet me at the airstrip and take me directly to the scene, lights on and siren blaring.

They had cordoned off the whole area front and back and the scene looked to be relatively unpolluted. I had not called my team yet as there was no confirmation the two murders were connected. That is, until I stepped around the corner into the hallway and saw the deceased on his back, a pool of blood around his head. I could immediately see that his nose had been destroyed and that was likely what had killed him.

The Coroner would confirm but I could see he was dead from a single, surgical strike up into the nose that drove the bones into his brain. He would have died almost instantly from such a blow. It was a telltale sign of such a blow when I saw blood had oozed from both eardrums as well as his nose.

As soon as I saw the wife, I directed all officers to clear the scene and maintain the perimeter. I let them know the FBI would be taking over.

She had bruises to her face and had obviously been hit, more than once. She admitted to passing out but nothing after that until she awoke in the morning looking for her "scumbag boyfriend".

Turns out he had laid hands on her far more often than this time. I called our forensics and crime analysis team in, and they were on a plane in an hour. There was no doubt of the connection, although I got the sense, we would not find any forensics to connect the two, other than my gut instincts.

Instincts never carried any weight in a court of law though, so we would need to be as thorough as always. We had to give those prosecutors absolutely as many facts and hard evidence as we could get to help them convict the guilty. I sometimes wondered about our whole legal system but that system, guided by jurisprudence, is all we have. We are obligated to rely on it and trust that it remains fair and equitable for all, even when sometimes it seems that is not the case.

Our people were on site quickly and while the local cops canvassed the neighborhood our team gathered evidence. One of the techs found a footprint close to a shed out back. He said it was about a size nine work-boot. The dead guy wore about a size twelve and the woman had little feet for a big girl. Perhaps it was useful? He took a plaster cast of the print just in case. All the evidence was gathered and catalogued.

We went to the local field office to start reviewing. The cast they had taken of the boot print produced some interesting information.

The forensic scientists have a program where you scan in the plaster mold of a footprint, add in things like the area, day or night, last time it rained and general soil type. The software then gives you an approximate weight of the person who left the footprint. It wasn't an exact science, but it could help provide some focus on who we were looking for. If you fed the software the right information it would give you a likely weight, plus or minus 10%. That was rather good, but you still had to watch for garbage in – garbage out. It was critical to get all the required data as accurate as possible to narrow down the weight range.

We now knew this perp was riding a motorcycle and wore size nine boots. Thanks to our crime lab, we also knew he weighed between 130 and 160 pounds. Not definitive to be sure but it would be easy to spot a small guy on a big bike. Or perhaps maybe even a woman... Maybe this case wasn't a loser after all! Having a weight range helped, especially when it was different than one would expect for the circumstances of the crime.

We also knew the killer was right-handed due to the angle of the blows.

We continued to canvass the area and, no surprise, nobody remembered much of anything out of the ordinary. I knew that eventually this guy would slip up though, they always did.

Two dead, the same type of blow killing each and both had hit women. It looked like he might be killing guys who were abusing women. I just needed to find out how he was picking them which would be no small task. It was a little too early for a profile but building an accurate one happens in various stages. We were still in stage one.

Still, as the case moved forward, I was confident there would be slip-ups and clues would be left behind. There always were.

Forensics now was a real science and the people working in that field had serious smarts. If something were left behind, they would find it. I always found their work fascinating, especially the way they would make fact-based deductions that helped lead to us to the right people. They sometimes started with only the tiniest shred of evidence but, the way their minds worked, they were then able to build on that one small piece. Oftentimes they delivered case-closing analysis of the evidence.

I had solved many cases solely due to the quality of the forensics. Sure, I had to tie everything together, but without the lab's efforts and hard work I would have been dead in the water. That was the way law enforcement was going these days, at least at my level.

Chapter Eleven – Where to Next?

I sat in my room upset with myself for getting caught unprepared like that. Any more mistakes and those pukes might be able to eventually identify me. Some FBI clown who had no idea what I have done in my life, how I have helped our country, or how good I was at my job might figure it out. I vowed I would NOT slip up again. I also decided I would take no innocents. Forget the coverup aspect. I would continue to implement my plan without taking one innocent life. It would have been against everything I believe in and fought for.

With that in mind, as I saw black SUV's driving around town that were clearly FBI, I decided I would lay very low for another couple of days. The place was busy enough I figured I could clear my mind with a good run and not get noticed. I got on my running gear, teed up the tunes, grabbed my hat and sunglasses and took off. I stashed my blond wig and other gear safely away in case the maids ignored the do not disturb sign and made up my room.

I ran past the crime scene on the adjacent street and saw it remained all taped off and there were a few cops still there. As I continued my run, I recalled having my gloves on during the attack. I knew there were no prints. I had already burnt the clothes and boots I was wearing and there was no other way to connect me.

Other than the fact this clown was killed with the same blow as the other one I was in the clear. These guys were indeed sharp if they figured that out so quickly. I chuckled as I thought, right they have Special Agent Sharpe on the case!

As I ran, I began to strategize on where best to go to give myself the most breathing room. I decided I would head back to Phoenix to find my next target. I would use forensic countermeasures to completely disguise the time of death and make it look like it happened before the first one. This would help throw them off my trail for a little while anyway, provided the countermeasures were not obvious. I knew I could pull that off, so I waited a couple more days and then packed up my bike and took off. Of course, I did a little clothes shopping at a couple of places along the way to replenish my supplies.

I rolled into Phoenix in the early afternoon looking for an out of the way motel that was close to a seedy area. It appeared there were a few of those but I settled on one down by the fairgrounds, which was also close to the airport. It was definitely not the best part of town. I found a hidden place to stash my bike and walked with my bags to the motel. I had my blond wig back on, a different baseball cap and my riding boots. I avoided the security camera as I checked in and paid with cash.

I walked down a dirty, dimly lit hallway to my room and turned the key in the lock. The place was so old they still used actual keys rather than swipe cards. As I opened the door, I was met with the stench of air freshener assaulting my senses.

Combined with the crunch of my boots with each step I really wished I could be somewhere else. That was not an option though as this appeared to be one of the "better" motels in this area. I also knew I could not draw attention to myself by checking out right after I checked in, that was a great way to get remembered.

Once in my room I immediately decided I would sleep fully clothed and perhaps even with a hat on. This joint was a real dump! Oh well, beggars couldn't be choosers and if I were to have long-term success, this would probably happen again. After all, it is easiest to remain unseen and unnoticed when you live among those who have been so for their whole life.

Many people here survived day to day. Some wearing rags and living in cardboard boxes for shelter, others living in cheap motels like this one. I felt sorry for them but for many this life was a choice; they had just checked out of mainstream society. They eliminated their own options and chose to live on the fringe of society.

I prepared to head over and find a bar where I was confident, based on the area, I would find at least one guy who needed to be taken out. I put a few things in my inside jacket pocket including a couple of nitrile gloves, a deerskin glove for my left hand and an aluminum tent peg. I realized I had finished the other two with a blow from my right hand and the next one needed to come from my left. Thankfully the government had been thorough enough to ensure I could kill equally well with either hand, or either foot or many other things for that matter.

So, I had the plan in place and had decided on my method. Now it was time to determine the who, the when and the where! As I walked into the dark bar and grabbed a beer, I realized the who was going to be quite easy in this place.

I quickly assessed a menagerie of dirt-bags, greaseballs, drunks and assorted other hooligans. Hell, it looked as if a fight might break out any second in this dump. It was a clientele I figured was typical for this area. I could find enough targets here to kill one a week for the next year, maybe two a week. And it wasn't even THAT large a bar!

I ultimately decided there were too many options and too many chances for problems. Combined with the likelihood of a police-visit-required altercation being high, I set my beer down and quietly left. After wiping off prints and any DNA that may have been on the bottle of course.

I had my lips coated with a clear sealer but better safe than sorry. I had also coated my fingers with a thin layer of silicone sealant that served to cover up fingerprints. It was a cheap but effective way to add protection in case a glove came off.

As I was walking to the next bar a couple of men started trying to talk to me. They were behind me mumbling all kinds of stupid things. I suppose that meant I fit in down here, which was a good thing. I kept on walking, ignoring them, and thanks to my speed and their drunkenness there was no contact. I certainly did not want to beat up a couple of drunks on the sidewalk, but I can tell you I was getting close to doing just that. I was glad to see that I was getting back to my old self, able to focus on the task at hand and keep my emotions in check.

I really wanted to just turn around and explain to them why they should not say things like that. Explain with my fists and feet of course. I calmed myself and kept going, quite content with my lack of response.

I only had to travel two more blocks to find the "right" bar, if we wish to call it that. It looked every bit as bad as the first one, but I hoped it had a slightly better clientele overall. Maybe there would be some close to regular folks in here. I was still confident there would be an abuser or two in here. It seemed there were altogether too many of those around.

It was very disconcerting that there just seemed to be so many men like this. How could their mothers and sisters have gone so wrong? What kind of father does not bring a young boy up to respect women?

Chapter Twelve – An Easy Kill

I surveyed the parking lot, the alley and the surrounding area and knew exactly where I would walk when I left. I entered the bar, identifying where the security cameras were and skillfully avoiding them. I sat at a table in yet another dark corner with my hat pulled low over my blond wig. I had on baggy jeans, another pair of work boots and two shirts. The overall effect made me look at least forty pounds heavier and twenty years older, exactly what I was going for. Combined with the glasses, I felt I could bump into my own mother, and she would have no idea it was me.

I knew that if I was able to finish someone in the darkened alley there was a grease trap out there. The base ph combined with the usual grease eating agents would quickly make the kill look much older than it was. The problem was there could be no connections to someone currently in the bar. Usually, police didn't check too far when one of these folks turned up dead anyway. They would likely report only the forensics and use that to determine time of death. The face would also be eaten away quickly, further compounding the problem of a solid ID, which would add more time. I was quite sure most of these people wouldn't have dental records either.

I waited and watched, realizing my plan may not come to fruition the first night. Sure enough, no opportunities presented themselves to me.

I slipped out of the bar and as I passed one of the alleys, I spotted a guy with what appeared to be a hooker. I tried to ignore it but then he slapped her and forced her to her knees in front of him. She was crying and trying to resist. I was close enough to hear him say if she bit him, she was dead. I decided I would let her clear the area before I disposed of this piece of garbage.

I really wanted to intervene sooner, but it was safer if I just let her walk away and then I could take him separately. No witnesses would HAVE to be my motto from here on. I knew the chances of a hooker saying anything were slim anyway, so I felt safe with the plan. It's not like the police usually had a ton of respect for those poor women. Too often crimes against them were not taken seriously. I would fix that, at least in this case.

I was disgusted as I heard her choke a bit and shortly after that heard him telling her to get the hell out of the alley and keep her mouth shut. She ran towards the street and thankfully turned away from me and headed the other direction. I had slipped on a nitrile glove inside of the deerskin glove and had a good grip of the tent spike in my left-hand jacket pocket. It was aligned with my forearm so that I could generate the maximum amount of power when I struck. It would be easier to accomplish if I was behind him, but I wanted to be looking into his eyes as I buried that spike into his brain.

I turned into the alley and quietly walked toward Mr. Romantic. I checked out all around to confirm we were alone. As I got closer to him, he asked who the hell I was. I just smiled and said he shouldn't have done that to her. He said it was none of my damn business and he started to move toward me. I stood my ground and let him approach me, which seemed to surprise him. I was confident he was not used to women who did not back down from him or cower in fear. He was clearly not smart enough to realize there may be a reason for my complete absence of fear. I stood quietly, assessing the situation as he approached closer.

When he was in the ideal position, I slipped my gloved hand out of my pocket and quickly drove the spike deep into his right ear. He made almost no sound as he collapsed and fell to the ground at my feet. He grabbed at my leg as I watched the life ooze out of him. I kicked his arm away and then had to see if there was a grease trap close and if I could get him to it cleanly. There were no other people around and minimal light, so I was good to go.

I spotted one only about fifteen yards away, following the sickening stench of ancient fry grease. I rolled up the deerskin glove inside out and slipped a nitrile glove onto my other hand. I used his own jacket to cover his head and keep the blood off me as I drug him over to the bin. There was a little blood on the ground but once I dumped him it wouldn't matter.

I left the spike in his head intentionally and threw him into the grease trap, face down. I knew that based on the angle of the blow and the fact it was into his right ear they would deduce the killer was left-handed. It would likely be at least three days, if not longer, by the time they found him. I would be long gone by then.

I got him tossed into the trap and used a hose to wash away any blood residue. It was a wet dirty alley anyway so the chances of anything being seen were slim, especially with the stockyards nearby.

There was an acrid stench everywhere in this alley, perhaps even the whole area, which overwhelmed the senses.

I gathered myself and strolled calmly back to my motel room. I took my boots and clothes I had on along with the gloves and sealed them all up into a baggie. Somewhere on the road I would have a small fire to ensure nothing could be recognized. I would check out early in the morning and get on the road.

As the sun rose, I packed up everything and loaded up my bike, anxious to see this squalid, sad area in my mirror. I rode slowly up to the freeway and proceeded calmly and lawfully back home. I felt peaceful leaving that town behind me and it was a nice ride home. That was the good thing running between Phoenix and LA. The roads were pretty much perfect, and the weather was almost always great for biking.

I stashed my bike in the garage and went inside to shower and wash off the road grime. After my night in that fleabag motel, I could not seem to scrub my skin hard enough. I got out, dried off and snuggled into my warm and cozy bed. I figured it was now time to lay low for a while.

I awoke the next morning, happy to be in my own bed. Compared to the last motel it was like sleeping in a cloud. I needed to destress and relax and work out. I made sure I was seen around the hood, running, getting groceries, working out etc. I always ran at the same time and the same route. I was always in the gym at the same time too. I knew that people would remember those sightings but not necessarily the exact dates. If they saw me enough during this time it would be easier to set up an alibi if I ever had to. In this case, there was something to be said for routine.

Eyewitnesses were never that reliable anyway and I only needed one or two to cast doubt should I ever need it. They were frequently confused about days and times and a judge or jury only needed to hear one or two competing witnesses to discount everything. It was somewhat counterintuitive to consider that routine and regularity would not help with eyewitnesses. The average person would think that the witness(es) would remember the one day you did not show and perhaps blow your alibi.

In the majority of cases, it was just the opposite though. Days and times would get confused and run together and that was the benefit of routine. Witnesses would often begin to question their own recollections and it did not take much to get people to second-guess themselves.

Chapter Thirteen – Tracking the Bad Guy

I was having my morning coffee back in my LA field office and reviewing recent murders and accidents in Arizona, California and New Mexico. I had seen nothing for a couple of weeks when I spotted a report out of Phoenix.

A guy had apparently been killed in an alley close to a dive bar by the stockyards. I have no idea why, but something made me keep reading. Turns out they found him in a grease trap and were claiming time of death was roughly a week before the first murder I was currently looking into.

As I read further, I discovered he had been killed with a tent spike. No other marks, no other blows. One deadly tent spike directly into his brain via the ear canal. I noted further details and kept a copy in my file. There was no reason to think there would be, but I wanted to find out if there were any other forensics. I felt this could be connected to my guy somehow and I would find that link if it existed.

I contacted Phoenix PD the next day and discussed the findings with the homicide detective in charge. They had virtually nothing to go on. It was a busy alley in a seedy area. I asked if they had spoken with any of the locals and they claimed they interviewed quite a few but without an accurate description it was tough.

I left him with a request to let me know if they ever came up with an ID or any information, he thought I might find useful. I had a good relationship with the Phoenix PD as they had helped me out on a few of my cases in the past. I found their detectives to be thorough, professional and always willing to go the extra mile. It was uncharacteristic, as us feds weren't exactly loved and respected by local police forces. Usually, they felt intimidated by us and cooperation, if not forced, did not exist. Nobody like anyone working on "their turf" and cutting in on local police business.

Darned if I didn't receive a call the very next day. One of their CI's had heard something about a hooker being assaulted in the very same alley, but it was not as long ago as they currently thought. The timelines didn't match up, so I asked where exactly the body was found in the grease trap.

He confirmed it was on the top of the mess, face down. Hmm, the chemicals in a grease trap could make a body look like it had been dead longer than it had been, which could skew a timeline. I got some more details and asked if he might be able to find that hooker and bring her in for questioning. I also asked if he would be kind enough to let me patch in via video and he said that would be no problem.

I got a call on my cell a couple of days later. They had the girl and were bringing her in now. Could I get to a conference call setup within an hour, or would I just do it on my phone? I raced back to the field office.

The phone was great in a pinch, but I wanted a big screen. I needed to be able to look into her eyes as she spoke. I wanted to be able to pick up any nuances or stress as she was being interviewed. I knew the local PDs were good at their jobs, but FBI agents had so much more training in this area. Reading a person, watching their facial clues and body language. All the things my wife did so well.

We got set up quickly and in no time, I was looking at a grey wall in the Phoenix PD interrogation room. The officer brought the girl in after the detective and I chatted briefly. She looked rough for sure. She was certainly not your high-class call girl. Nevertheless, nobody had any right to treat another human being the way she had been treated.

Too often people like her were completely disregarded with many thinking they simply did not count. I knew the Phoenix PD did not think that way from our previous interactions. They clearly understood how it was supposed to be, all lives having equal value in the eyes of the law. Every citizen entitled to protection and the opportunity to live their own life how they saw fit. The USA was founded on those principles, and we would do everything we could to uphold them.

She said she was on her way to visit a friend when she decided on a short cut through the alley. She knew the area well and wasn't too concerned.

As she was walking past a bar this guy stepped out of the shadows and stopped her asking for a freebie. She tried to get away but couldn't and ended up being forced to give him what he wanted. She said she did what she was told and then ran out of the alley.

The detective asked if she saw or noticed anyone else before or after. She said she had not seen a thing other than his face. She just wanted to get away as quickly as possible. We reconfirmed the actual date she said it had happened and there was no doubt in my mind she was telling the truth.

The detective showed her a rendering of the dead guy done through facial reconstruction and she immediately said that's him. Have you got him? I hope someone kicked his ass. The detective then told her he was found dead in that same alley. She just smiled saying it was great to get another jerk off the street. It was a completely normal and expected reaction from a woman in her position. She had already seen far too much in her young
life.

We knew there was no way it was this girl but now we had a new timeline and different questions to ask. Once she was clear I asked the detective to re-canvass the area and ask specifically if anyone spotted someone on a big Harley.

The analysis of the tire track from the first crime scene had turned up a style of tire and tread that was unique to Harley Davidson. The weight also matched with the larger Harley's versus other pretenders. Your bigger Harley weighs upwards of nine hundred pounds before they were loaded. I now knew what type of bike it was. A small clue, but when you add all the small clues together in cases like this you frequently solved the case. Still, we had no description, we still didn't even know if we were looking for a man or a woman. Problem is there are lots of Harleys around Phoenix! I felt it was worth a try anyway and the local detective agreed.

After we disconnected, I started to build the timeline differently and looked at who was killed where and our best estimate why. The first one was the Mexican guy who was killed west of Phoenix after someone saw him hitting his wife. The second one was a guy in Albuquerque who had abused his wife/girlfriend and apparently even raped her when she was out cold. What we now knew was the third and not the first kill was a guy that had abused a hooker.

So, we were definitely dealing with someone that took great issue with a man abusing and hitting women. Each one of these guys certainly deserved to be punished but murder was murder and vigilantes cannot be tolerated in a lawful society. It was up to us to catch the bad guys and the courts to decide their fate.

That was the reality that law enforcement people had to live with, and the parameters we were forced to work within, every day. Sometimes we did everything right, testified well, presented all the evidence but still lost the case. On those days, it was a real challenge to like or respect criminal defense lawyers. After a loss, I never understood how a prosecutor could shake the hand of a lawyer who had just gotten a guilty criminal released.

There were little to no forensics except for one boot print and a weight estimate from that print. Nobody had seen this person or persons at all. The first two were killed with single blows by a right-handed person. This was someone either trained in the martial arts or with serious military experience.

This last fellow was killed by a left-handed person using a readily available and impossible to track tent spike. I was starting to wonder if this was a connection or simply a coincidence. There were precious few people who were truly ambidextrous, and I figured a miniscule percentage of those would be killers. I could not begin to calculate those odds. I was just never that good at math. I compiled all the information, completed the timeline and closed the file on my desk. I needed a break and had to get out of there.

I went home to a nice hot dinner with my beautiful wife. Once we were done, I asked her if she felt like discussing a case.

She was an accomplished profiler and I wanted to get her thinking about this one for me. We opened a bottle of wine and sat out on the patio to chat about it. I laid everything out and she reminded me that she usually worked with direct evidence. She then gave the usual caveats I got during these "discussions". I said, "yeah, yeah I get it" and we both chuckled.

She went on to describe that this person perhaps watched his mother suffer serious abuse at the hands of a man. He may even have deep self-loathing because he himself abused women. He might be taking his revenge out on himself by killing those who resembled him. This would allow him to take many more of these abusers off the street rather than killing himself and therefore removing only one. Sick minds did not function like yours or mine do. They often have a skewed sense of moral justice and, in many cases, uncontrollable urges. Yes, some even hear little voices in their heads. Really.

I couldn't believe how Patti could stomach the information she studied for a living, but she was exceptionally good at her job. She stressed that these were extremely sick minds, and her craft was part science, part intuition and mostly guessing at the end of the day. Yes, the guesses were based on factual information and volumes of psychological study, but they were hypotheses, nonetheless.

Based on the possibly lighter weight I asked if it may perhaps be a woman. Patti highlighted that it was only recently that people started believing that women could be serial killers. For the longest time it was assumed women just "didn't have it in them". Today we know that around 12% of serial killers are in fact women.

She went on to say that it is likely even higher than that because women almost always act alone and plan meticulously. They get caught less frequently than males who are often more concerned about making a name for themselves. The males often want to be famous, but most all are relegated to infamy.

Psychology today had some very interesting female serial killer trivia. They noted a few myths and facts about female serial killers. The most popular myth was that there were no female serial killers. This was stated as late as 1998 by an FBI profiler. That magazine then confirmed 12% of all serial murders in the USA are committed by females.

Another myth was that a female was usually the subservient one on a male/female team. Again, not the case, although females tend to work alone more often anyway. There are other fallacies circulating including those related to the looks of a female serial killer and that they are simply man-haters.

Patti went on to say that the fact they operate alone more often means they are much more difficult to catch. She also mentioned that female serial killers typically killed within a gender role where they worked, such as nursing and teaching. Female serial killers tend to kill for power or money and not often domination or sexual violence.

These facts reduced the possibility I was seeking a female, which was good because they typically avoided capture twice as long males. Add to that, females usually kill with poison and that their profiles are eerily "normal", and it added up to a possible career-breaker for me.

She smiled and told me to watch the sun set on that beautiful Pacific Ocean and highlighted that we were done with "business" for the evening. Patti always knew when to cut off the work talk. I was not as good at that as she was. It seemed my mind never stopped when I was on a case. She could always tell when I was running through scenarios in my head no matter how hard I tried to keep it from her. I suppose that is one of the skills that makes her so good at her job.

We sipped our wine as the sun set and we made love by the pool as we sometimes did. The neighbors couldn't see anything, and you couldn't see from the beach either and we both liked doing it out there.

We loved our neighborhood and each day felt fortunate we were able to live in such a great area with a beautiful house right on the ocean.

Sure, the people next door and a few houses down the beach were party animals but that wasn't the end of civilization. Besides Kathy and Jonathon invited us over there a lot, so there were some perks too. They threw the best parties and we always liked going over there. They were all fun people.

Personally, I think they invited us because they knew I was in law enforcement and an ounce of prevention might be worth a pound of cure.

I told them more than once that the FBI doesn't get involved in this type of thing anyway, so they had no worries. When we were alone, they were always joking about me having pull with the local police and being able to short circuit any issues. I explained if anything, local law enforcement would rather bust our chops than give us a break. Local law enforcement never liked "the feds" of any sort.

Kathy, Jon, Angela and Luke were fun to be around though, and we didn't often turn down an invite to either house. We had them to our place a few times too, but I liked their yards a lot more than ours! Being at their home was like being in a different world. It was like you owned your own private slice of the beach and the ocean. Once you were in their houses or backyard you did not even notice they had neighbors.

Both had done very well for themselves but never let their wealth go to their heads. They were simply nice folks.

Chapter Fourteen – Just Hanging Around the House

I had planned to just lay low for a few weeks and stay out of everyone's way. On further reflection though, I had determined it might be safer to step up my social life while I was here. I needed to get out and about more often and do more things. I had to force myself to be around people more often and just hang out.

I gave Kathy a call and we chatted for quite a while. She said they were having a bunch of people over and I confirmed Bobby was not going to be there before I agreed to attend. I made it sound like I wanted to see him when I asked the question. When she said he wasn't coming I faked a "that's too bad" and left it at that. She said they hadn't seen him in a month anyway, so my plans were cemented.

I was planning not to drink but if I did, I could just roll my bike into the garage, so I decided to ride over. I had a bag with me with some clothes and a bathing suit and threw it into my saddlebag. As I was riding over, I realized I still had the New Mexico plate on, but then I had no reason to be concerned at that point. It was a beautiful day and I rolled up to their house, hopped off my bike and went inside. When I got in Kathy told me I was staying over so I should roll my bike into the garage now. I grudgingly agreed and went through the house, opened the garage and tucked my bike in next to their Porsche SUV.

It was early but there were already people milling around. I had met some at earlier gatherings and others were new. Kathy took me over to meet their neighbors, Colin and Patti. They were about the same age as us and seemed nice. We shook hands and chatted briefly. He looked familiar, but I couldn't place the face. I don't recall seeing them again until much later.

Colin came up and said Kathy told him I ride a Harley and he asked what type. I said it was a big bike and he said he didn't want to insult me but was it easy for anyone to ride those? I asked what he meant. He clarified that he was interested to know if shorter, lighter people could handle such a big motorcycle. I told him size meant nothing as once you got a Harley moving, they handled the same for everyone. Big or small, short or tall everyone was the same once the bike was rolling. It was a question anyone might ask, and I didn't give it another thought until something else came to light.

Later, Kathy said that Colin enjoyed talking to me and she said he was an FBI guy and that was when it hit me. THAT was why he seemed familiar. This was the same Colin who was working on my case. At first, I was immediately scared and a little flustered but soon decided that this would now be an even greater challenge. Could I outsmart the vaunted FBI right under their very nose? I was sure I could, as I had worked unidentified right in the back yards of some of the most respected and dangerous police forces, special forces and gang territories in the world.

Still, I looked at his earlier question from an unfamiliar perspective now. Of course, I would need to be even more careful. I suddenly flashed back to my bike downstairs. I knew I couldn't say anything, but I hoped and prayed the bike was not mentioned again. I certainly did NOT want to go down and show it to him, especially with the New Mexico plate still attached.

I vowed to go to the DMV the next day, claim my plate was stolen and get a new California one. By saying the plate was stolen I would have another backstop plus I would not need to have the out-of-state registration inspection which might create a paper trail. I remember parking next to the SUV which hid my bike from view. Of course, there was no way Kathy and Jonathon would let anyone leave through the garage anyway, so I needn't worry.

I planned to get the new plate, park my bike in my own garage and find a good deal on a used bike. I could pay with cash, register under an alias and use my fake driver's license to keep it all under the radar. Maybe one of those Honda touring bikes that went fast like an ST 1300 or something. After all, you meet the nicest people on a Honda they say. Who would ever look for a killer on one of those?

Okay, I was able to relax a bit. When I saw Colin leave with his wife I could really relax.

I was still a little bit shaken though and started thinking about his question. Was it an innocent question, just seeking general knowledge or did he have reason to believe the killer was a smaller man? Or perhaps a woman? He might be narrowing down WHO to look for, but I was confident he had no idea WHERE to look, at least for the moment.

He may even have figured out the WHY at this point, but I felt that was a good thing. Perhaps men might start to realize that abusing a woman should never happen. I wished that part of the story would show up in the news. The type of man who hit women needed to know there was a possibility of payback. They needed to understand the type of justice I could deliver.

It seems to have taken our society far too long to realize and accept that women and men should be treated as equals. One group should not be able to wield power over the other. One group should not be viewed as more "valuable" than the other. The equal pay thing has been big in LA for a while, but this is so much more than that.

I honestly don't personally care if some guy makes a few million more for doing a movie than an equivalent female star. Yes, I don't like the inequality of it, but they all get paid way too much for being pretty or sexy and having a good memory.

Chapter Fifteen – Time for A New Bike

The next week I scoured the auto trader looking for the right motorcycle. Luckily, I found a couple of options within a half hour of each other. I got my blond wig on and my average girl outfit and took off. Each time I looked in the mirror I was surprised at how different I looked in this getup.

Normally I never rode without a helmet but due to the wig I would ride in a baseball cap today. I had made appointments to see both bikes and was anxious to get going. I knew the ST 1300 was a popular bike and there were always lots on the road. I tapped into the DMV database and was able to confirm the most popular color by far was burgundy. There were literally hundreds and hundreds of them registered in California alone.

The first bike was mechanically sound with low kilometres but had custom paint. The guy that owned it thought it was just awesome, but I knew it would not work for me. Even without the paint the exhaust system was custom and louder than stock. Odd to find on a Honda and unique was not my goal. If I were just a rider, I probably would have liked it. But I wasn't just a rider, I needed to blend into the background where I was, not stand out. I thanked him for his time and went on my way.

Fortunately, the second bike was stock burgundy. The lady was selling it for her husband. It had very low miles on it and was priced right. It had the larger saddlebags and a rear seat with a bar on which

I could carry more luggage. I arranged to pick it up the next day, after a lien check and said that I would pay in cash. I briefly contemplated using a car, but I preferred to be on a motorcycle. They were easier to hide and provided much better handling if a getaway was ever needed.

I fully embraced the motorcycle when a big Ducati helped me escape certain death on a mission in Italy years ago. Had I have been in a car I was sure I would have been caught and killed. The maneuverability of the motorcycle and its quickness allowed me to go places cars could not. I was able to dart between traffic, down skinny alleys and across fields to easily escape my pursuers. From that point on you could say I was a true motorcycle aficionado. I know my Harley wasn't even remotely as agile as the Ducati or any other sport bike, but I had to consider the cool factor too.

I took a cab over with my riding gear and picked up the bike as arranged. We sat at her kitchen table while I counted out the cash. I had it in bank packs of 50 one-hundred-dollar notes. The deal was for a flat ten thousand, so we removed each strap and counted the bills into piles of ten. I wanted no confusion and no reason for anyone to think anything was odd. I told her I had come straight from the bank because most people preferred cash.

I had taken it for a quick blast up the coast and knew I had the right bike. If I ever did have to run, I would be able to do so on this bike. It was also such an "average" bike that I knew it wouldn't stick out in people's minds.

It wasn't quite as good as driving a black model T when that was the only car on the road, but it would be anonymous enough. Also, being more a dual-sport bike the ST1300 had the off-road capability to go with its speed and handling. It turned out to be in great shape and thanks to the low miles I knew I could ride it for a while without having to do any work on it.

I rode home and gave it a thorough going over in my garage. There were a few subtle changes I would make to give it even more power but, generally speaking, it was ready to go.

To be honest, I would have preferred a big Ducati, but they were very distinctive, and loud too, so that knocked them out of the running.

Chapter Sixteen – Setting Up the Alibi

I stuck to my plan and my schedule religiously. Running, training, spending time with friends. I even went back to Kathy and Jonathon's the next week. We hung out and chatted all day. Angie and Luke showed up and it was like old times, minus one. Luckily, I didn't have to mention Bobby as Jonathon said he had seen him with a new woman a few times. I smiled warmly and said, "good for him that's great."

I went on to say what a great guy I thought he was but wondering in my head if he had revealed his true self to the new girl yet? I said nothing and none of them had any reason to believe ours wasn't just a regular split and we had gone our separate ways. I was sure he would never divulge that I was the one that left. That would be too big a hit to his fragile little ego.

It was good to relax, but I soon started feeling the itch to get out and find another bad guy. To ensure I would be off the radar when I took out Bobby, I decided I need to find someone else in California. Not too close to home but in the same state at least. The next time I was over at Kathy's I made a point of letting everyone know I was taking off on a ride to Palm Springs and Indio for a long weekend.

The next weekend I rode up to Palm Springs on my Honda and I must admit I really did like the way it handled. Nice curvy roads once you got closer to the mountains, it was great. It was a smooth, flat road winding its way through the hills. The black asphalt almost as perfect as the day it was laid. The Honda was also nice and quiet, so I knew you could start it and ride away without attracting attention, certainly much more quietly than on my Harley. It was an average, nondescript bike that would not stand out.

I knew I could get to Palm Springs and back quickly and easily. Due to the high volume of traffic, I would not be too easy to spot. It was only a little more than one hundred miles, so I wouldn't have to race either. Just a nice, leisurely drive that would not draw any attention.

I packed and left early the next day to ensure I would be seen in a restaurant or two, get noticed checking into a motel and later going into my room to sleep. I had decided the most likely place to find a target, amongst the too many options in and around LA would be El Monte or Downey. Either place someone who looked at least partially Mexican like me would fit in easily and disappear in the crowd. It was the hiding in plain sight concept, and I always found it worked well.

I got to Palm Springs, had lunch and lingered at the restaurant for a while. I chatted with the waiter enough that he would remember seeing me if he were ever asked.

A sangria and then a few glasses of water and I was good. I paid with my credit card and off I went to see if I could check in early.

The hotel I chose was close to the highway. It was a nondescript motel style that offered multiple access points to the rooms. There was a spot I could leave my bike at on the end of the building that would allow me to come and go without being noticed. It was the ideal location from which to implement my plan. The desk clerk was helpful and as I slid my credit card over, I asked for two nights. I walked with a limp by putting a stone in my boot and that was my reason for a ground floor room. I saw no reason to let him know I was riding a motorcycle. Also, the limp would likely be remembered and would throw off all but the best profilers.

I got my workout gear on and spent an hour and a half in the gym. I had a great workout and felt like a million bucks. I took an afternoon nap and then went to the restaurant up the street where I again used my credit card. All this was the real me, no wig, no disguise and my credit card was used in a few places. I wanted to be seen and seen a lot. I woke up close to six PM and started getting prepared. I could easily get out of my room without being seen and did not have to ride or walk past the office.

When it came time to leave, I hung the do not disturb sign on my door and then climbed out the bathroom window. I couldn't risk being seen leaving my room.

Luckily, I was at the back of the hotel and being a corner room there was little chance of me being spotted. I had on my big girl clothes, my blond wig and brought a baseball cap with me. I also had on my non-prescription glasses that would further hide my identity. I hopped on my bike around eight, silently rolled down the hill, fired it up and hit the highway.

It was a pleasant ride back into town as most traffic was going the opposite direction. I was in El Monte in no time and knew I had the right bar based on the vehicles I saw in the parking lot. There were some rough looking cars including a few half-completed low rider customs. I knew those cars well. Dingle balls around the windows, skinny lake-pipes, and electric adjustable shocks. Those cars were real works of art with expensive paint jobs and the ground illuminated from the undercarriage. Most had mags that had spinner hubcaps on them so when the car stopped next to you the wheels looked like they were still moving. To be honest, the parking lot looked like a Cheech & Chong movie.

There was a free parking area for the stores in the next block, so I parked my bike there instead, away from all the lights. I wasn't sure I would find a target tonight, but I was prepared to make the two-way ride once or twice more to ensure my cover. I shouldn't have worried. This place was a real hole, and it was loaded with pukes. I never understood why women would put up with the crap they put up with, but I had already spotted a couple here. I wasn't worried about this kill at all.

As a matter of fact, I wanted Detective Sharpe to hear about it. This was the best way to solidify my alibi. After all, I was up in Palm Springs the whole weekend!

I had my blond wig, the right makeup, my big girl clothes and my glasses. Even if I was spotted, there was no way I would be identified. I looked the part of the typical trashy girl one might see in this area. Black bra underneath a white T-shirt, boots and jeans. I fit in very well to say the least.

I paid for a beer with cash and just sat there. I had a couple of guys come my way, but I think my look scared them off. I watched and waited and there, two tables away, was just the type of guy I was looking for. He was belittling his woman and even in the noisy bar I could hear him call her a "stupid C%#$" more than once. I HATED that word and decided without delay if he raised a hand to her, he would be the one. I looked them both over closely. Clothes that seemed to have not seen a laundry in a week of being worn, messy hair and dirty faces. He had a scraggly beard to finish off his "look".

It wasn't too long after when I again heard him call her that disgusting name and saw him grab her arm. He was obviously hurting her and would not let go. He said something into her ear and out they went. I slipped out the side door, taking my beer bottle and dumping it into the overflowing trash outside. I planned to follow them at a safe distance.

As I came around the front of the bar, I could see they were not in a vehicle. It appeared they were walking home and that was ideal for me. He was abusive the whole way and I decided he had to suffer a little bit before I removed him from this earth.

Only a couple of blocks away they turned down a street and I watched as they entered a tiny house. They both seemed very drunk at this point. I snuck around to the back and was able to see into a messy living room through a cracked, hazy window. They had drinks already and he was all over her. You could tell she had already separated from herself and whatever he was going to do she was going to let him. I wanted to catch them unaware, and I would prefer if he was alone, so I waited. He used her body for his own pleasure as she cried and when he was done, she left. I was able to see her go to the bedroom after that, and she quickly passed out as he sat there staring blankly at the TV.

I let myself in silently through the back door and waited next to the fridge. The house was disgusting top to bottom. I was glad I was wearing gloves as there didn't appear to be a clean surface anywhere. Only a couple of dim yellowed bulbs lit the room, but I could still see dead bugs on the floor close to the baseboards. They no doubt got stuck to the floor trying to get back to their dark, moldy homes in the walls.

I suppose I should not have been surprised at the state of the house based upon the condition of the people living in it. I waited patiently on the other side of the fridge. I knew he would come for another beer soon and when he did, I would immobilize him.

A few minutes later he came around the corner and I disabled him quietly with a quick blow to the throat. I caught him before he hit the floor, gagged him and then zip-tied him to a chair. I nearly got sick to my stomach maneuvering him into the chair as being that close to him the stench was unbearable.

I wasn't ever really into torture, but I decided this clown was different. I wanted him to survive for a while to think about what he had done.

I sat in front of him and undid his belt and then pulled down his jeans and underwear. I watched his eyes as I pulled my knife out of my boot. It was your typical, army surplus straight blade knife. I had honed it myself so that you could split hairs if you were good enough.

I gave him some time to realize what I was about to do as I twirled the blade in my hand. His eyes got wide, and he tried to scream but he was effectively gagged. He struggled against the ties to free himself but there was zero chance of him breaking free. I told him he was a pig, and I was doing this for the girl in the other room.

I took my gloved hand and pulled that disgusting thing away from his body. I held it out straight and brought the razor-sharp blade across it quickly at the base and cut him off cleanly as he screamed into the gag. I threw it on the floor at his feet.

He was bleeding profusely, as alcohol thins the blood, and I knew he would be gone in minutes. I let him sit there and watch the life run out of his body onto the grimy floor. I turned my shirt inside out, put my jacket back on and wiped off my jeans. I went quietly out the back door, cleaning myself with wet wipes as I went and taking everything with me. I stuffed the wipes into a bag in my jacket and moved down the alley and back to where I had parked my bike. I rode calmly and quietly back to Palm Springs, stashed my bike exactly where it had been and climbed back into my room.

I removed any bloody clothes and stuffed them into the zip lock bags along with the wipes. I went into the shower but before doing so used bleach and a toothbrush and then a sharpening stone to completely clean my knife of all evidence. The stone and the knife would be tossed into a river along the way and would never be found. I would have another roadside campfire with the balance of the evidence.

I had a long, hot shower and when I emerged, I was calm in the knowledge that I was doing the right thing.

I had completed another successful operation. One more bad guy no longer walking around looking for women to hurt. I wasn't happy about how I had done it but was glad it was done.

I left as I had arrived, no trace that I had ever been in El Monte. I had a great ride back to my hotel. I stopped at a roadside picnic area, lit a small fire in the fire pit and burned the baggies full of evidence. I stayed until I was certain everything was reduced to ashes and then rode off.

I woke up the next morning after I had stashed everything safely and walked down to the office to ask about a good restaurant for breakfast. I already knew but wanted to ensure I was seen in the early AM, looking rested and revived. I went over to the restaurant, made enough small talk to be remembered by my waitress, ate and left.

I got back to my room, put my running gear on with my yoga style shorts and a cropped top. No hat, just that outfit and sunglasses and I went on a nice long run. It was great running up here. The weather was always good and with the tunes blasting in my earphones it seemed I could run forever.

I had a great run and felt raring to go after another shower. I toured Palm Springs for the day, grabbing a date shake of course. I then had a nice lunch followed by a light dinner and went to catch a movie. The theatre was close to the hotel, so I could just walk over.

There was some action flick playing and that was right up my alley. A bag of popcorn, bottle of water and I was good to go.

The sun had already set when I walked back to my room, but it was still nice and warm, and the air smelled clean. I had another great sleep that night. In the morning I went to the front desk to check out and then had an uneventful ride back home. I got home in the early afternoon after a very pleasant ride back through the hills. I even stopped a couple of times just to admire the scenery, acres of evergreens painting the smooth rolling hills with various shades of green.

I put my Honda in my garage, jumped on my Harley and headed over to Kathy's directly to "drop in". I wanted them to see me on my Harley and tell them how much fun I had in Palm Springs. They didn't even know I had another bike anyway and I wanted it to stay that way. Luckily, she and Jonathon were both at home. I parked out front, California plates back on my bike, and went in for a while.

I didn't stay too long but wanted to make sure my weekend away was imprinted on their memories. We chatted about how great the ride was and how much we loved the high desert.

Kathy mentioned they had a place in Palm Springs, and I could have just stayed there. I was glad I was only hearing that now as it would look strange if I opted to stay in a hotel when I could have stayed for free. I needed the hotel to build my alibi to ensure it was supported by multiple people.

My very next thought was "how rich are these people"? They have a beach front mansion, but they need another house in Palm Springs...why? Need to get away from the perfect view? Tired of the cool sea breezes blowing through your home? Sick of walking on the soft white sand as the sun sets over the Pacific?

Sometimes people with money just seemed so far out there!

Chapter Seventeen – Safely Back Home

I rode back home, washed both bikes in my garage and went inside to relax. The news came on at five and I was watching to see if anything was reported. There was close to a murder a day in the city of Los Angeles alone, many times they didn't even make the news. I was not completely surprised to see that mine did though. After all, it wasn't every day that a murder was so brutal, even around Los Angeles. Bad ones like this were more a monthly occurrence.

The news reported a grisly murder where a man was apparently tortured while his wife slept in the next room. In this town that wouldn't necessarily make mine the only one but when they showed the guy's face it was clear. He still had what could best be described as a terrified look on his face. That was how I wanted him to die, scared, just like the women he had no doubt been terrorizing for most of his life.

These guys didn't just start this behaviour out of nowhere. They were usually the ones torturing small animals and beating up others when they were little. He was the kid with the magnifying glass burning the legs off spiders and then watching as they tried to escape.

In many cases they were either the bully in school or the one getting bullied. Either way, they were damaged individuals. But, no matter what your upbringing, you still had choices that could be made. They could choose not to hit women the way their fathers most likely did. Instead, they just perpetuated the cycle.

Inside I was happy that he died feeling just as his wife or girlfriend had likely felt her whole life. He had to sit there and watch as the life dripped slowly from his body, the roaches and bugs gathering to feast. I hope he was smart enough to get the irony of the whole situation, but I didn't really care. Whether he understood why or not, wasn't my concern. I just knew there was one more bad guy off the streets.

I figured I now had to lay low for quite a while and keep up with my usual life. Running, training and just living. I would see the girls at the gym where we would chat and plan our next outing. Both Kathy and Angela were starting to tease me again about being the fifth wheel. They regularly asked if they could introduce me to someone. I just said that I really wasn't interested right then. I know they were just trying to help a friend, but it was starting to get a little tiring. They let me know they were having a big party, this weekend, to which I was invited. I made them promise no setups or special introductions before telling them I'd love to attend.

I was good with that and was excited to meet some new people and just hang out. As usual, it was an afternoon start. The theme was some sunset-watching or something like that. They always seemed to need some sort of theme. I will admit that I could watch the sun set over the waves of the Pacific every evening and never tire of it. Watching the golden hued rays reflecting off the gentle evening waves always relaxed me. I have even surfed at dusk a few times but that is a dangerous thing to do so I had not done it often. Sharks were often active at dusk, and I had no desire to get in a scrap with one or two of those. They were not fights that humans typically won.

As usual, I was the first one there and the three of us were soon out on the patio getting some sun. I was back to my favorite, athletic, keep-me-mostly-covered bathing suit and the girls were both in tiny bikinis as usual. They seemed so at home displaying what appeared to be 95% of their skin. I guessed it was a California thing because there were definitely a lot of tiny bikinis.

The first people to arrive after me turned out to be Special Agent Sharpe and his wife. Geez! I wasn't ready for that, but I was trained to remain cool under ANY circumstances. I shook hands, said hi again and noticed the two of them looked rather good too. They were dressed differently the first time we met. Go figure, another good-looking California couple.

I wasn't sure whether they were all born here or if they moved here once they realized they were more of the beautiful people. It seemed like that was a prerequisite to own one of these spectacular beachfront mansions.

Patti was wearing a one piece with enough cut outs and holes that she might as well have been wearing a bikini. Colin was just wearing some board shorts with an open shirt, and I determined he was in better shape than your average FBI dude.

A lot of those agents got fat and slow after five or ten years on the job unless they were on a special detail. I preferred to stay away from the

FBI, but it was comforting to know that it would likely take three of them at once to have even a slim chance at taking me down. Perhaps only two Colins?

The whole bureau was filled with brainiacs anyway. They had been taught basic self defense and knew just enough to get themselves hurt if they were ever in a real fight. They were trained well in shooting though. I supposed they were good at taking bullets for Presidents and talking into their wrist mics but that was about it as far as I could tell. I had not seen too many that I thought would pose a threat to me. In fact, I don't think I'd break a sweat taking out any of them, at least one on one.

We all shook hands and Patti said it was nice to see me again. Colin smiled and asked me how the riding was going? I said just great asking him how he was doing. I told them about Palm Springs and what a great ride it was.

He said he was on a case that was really stretching him, but he never really talked about that stuff out of work. I smiled and said, "if you ever do want to talk, I would love to hear about it." Patti just rolled her eyes and begged me not to get him started. I went on to explain how much I loved mysteries and true crime type stories and he said, "yeah, this is true crime all right." I left it at that as I did not want to look too interested. It always raised red flags when anyone tried to insert themselves into an investigation. I did however want to get his take on this if I could, so I was hoping my prompting might produce some results later.

More people arrived and there were plenty of opportunities for S A Sharpe to share details of his case, but he was true to his word. There was no more talk about it.

As usual, it was an eclectic group of people and there were always interesting folks to meet. One of the neighbors up the beach the other way was a unique couple.

I was sure they were hippies, actual hippies, who were now in their late sixties. He still surfed and had long gray hair that he liked to keep in a ponytail. He had a few tattoos that were now barely recognizable due to a combination of saggy skin, age of the tattoo and way too much sun. He was a blast to chat with though and I always found myself talking to them at each party. His name was Arlo and hers was Sage. They could have been Sonny and Cher or Zappa and Sparrow, any names of that type would have worked for them. They were just priceless and SO Californian.

If you looked up the definition of "flower child" in the dictionary you should see a picture of Sage. I had now met them at a few of these gatherings and had never seen her in anything else but denim shorts and one of those cottony peasant shirts.

As the sun started to drop lower in the evening sky, she decided to go in the water. Arlo watched intently as she stood at the edge of the shore dropped her shorts, took off her top and in she went. No bathing suit, no underwear, just wearing what she was born with. Arlo just smiled at me and said Sage loved swimming naked, reminded her of the Woodstock days.

No surprise there I thought. I was sure they were front and centre at a place like that and certainly higher than kites.

From a distance she seemed in surprisingly good shape, and I had to think she was a yoga nut or something. I thought it was cute the way he seemed unable to take his eyes off her as she strolled naked into the surf. Arlo and I chatted a bit more about nothing in particular. When Sage came out of the water, I said we could talk more later as he walked over to her with a towel. I had already seen enough and didn't really need a closeup view.

We all just hung out, had a few drinks and snacks, and enjoyed what it means to live in Southern California. Beaches, beautiful people and lots of sun and sand. As the sun sank lower into the horizon the colors were amazing, the waves illuminated by the setting sun. You could see far up the beach with shuttered lifeguard stands darkly silhouetted against the fiery sky. On almost every one of them you could see a couple, legs dangling, most making out, as they too watched the orange sun move slowly lower before sinking silently into the ocean.

Once it was fully set people began to migrate from the sand to the swimming pool and the hot tubs. They had one tub built into the pool and a second one down on the lower deck. The lower deck tub was one of those original redwood hot tubs, complete with barrel staves and wooden benches around the edge. They were so cool, a real throwback to the golden age in Southern California. This was the birthplace of the hot tub as far as I knew. It was definitely the origin of these redwood tubs; of that I was certain.

When you were in that redwood tub looking out at the ocean you felt like you were back in the fifties or sixties. It was the heyday for the Southern California lifestyle. I understood Arlo and Sage a little better after a soak in that tub, easily imagining myself in that era.

Jon and Kathy had been running around delivering all kinds of drinks to those of us who found it difficult to leave the warm embrace of those tubs for even a minute. It was all good and another great gathering. I expected nothing less as whether we were at Kathy and Jon's, or Angela and Luke's an enjoyable time was always had by all.

This WAS Southern California.

Chapter Eighteen – The Detective's Take

I decided I was spending too much time in the LA field office so had taken to doing a little touring every now and then when I saw an interesting crime pop up. This day I found myself heading over to the El Monte PD to chat with an officer Diaz. I had worked with him a few years back and quite liked him.

He loved his job, was a hard worker and a smart guy. I told him more than once I thought he would make a great FBI agent. He always shrugged it off saying he prefers real police work rather than opening someone's mail all day. Ouch! I still liked him though and his sense of humour and had really enjoyed working with him.

It was always good to find local law enforcement that liked to work with us feds. They seemed few and far between, so I went out of my way to nurture relationships like this. If I could help them I most certainly would. I always watched for opportunities to pass something along that would build me up some credit.

I walked into the office and was met by Diaz and a nice hot cup of Starbucks. He did have a good memory. A large Americano with just a bit of milk.

We bro-hugged and said how great it was to see each other and then we headed over to his office. He had been promoted to detective since we last met. I congratulated him and said he was one step closer to the bureau. Of course, he just laughed it off.

I found it a little odd, but El Monte PD detectives each had their own small offices. Most police forces just kept an open pit where all the detectives sat at their desks. Desks piled high with file folders and papers, sticky notes everywhere and the mandatory coffee cup sitting next to a phone. Even the bureau was like that until you got into the higher ranks.

We were just sitting there yakking and he asks if I had heard about the murder there a couple of weeks ago? I laughed and said, "Which one, you guys are trying to take over the title from LA it seems." He didn't seem impressed with that comment, obviously I had struck a sore spot. I suppose none of us liked being accused of not closing enough cases.

We talked about that for a while and then he told me about this dirt-bag who had been killed in his own home. "Wait for it", he says. "The perp even cut off the guy's unit and left it at his feet while he bled out." "Really" I said, wondering if there was a connection to my active case. I asked him if it were his case and if so, could he grab the files? I went on to tell him about the case I was working, sharing as much as I could, and then he got the files from his cabinet.

I'm not shocked or floored by much anymore but I will admit the first photo he pulled out of the file did catch me by surprise. I swear that I felt a twinge in my own groin when I saw this guy's unit on the ground at his feet in a pool of blood. You could even see the tiny bugs grabbing a meal, immortalized in the crime scene photo. There's a job I would never want.

Diaz started to lay out the details and the more he talked the more interested I became. Certainly, the method of death was different than my guy but when he added the wife was in the other room passed out and bruised my spidey-senses again started tingling.

The crime scene photos showed everything. The zip ties were wide ones, like the police used. You could effectively restrain someone without cutting them or cutting off blood flow. We ended up agreeing that there were enough similarities that we should keep in touch. I asked him for a copy of the file which he graciously shared.

I knew what Patti and I would be discussing sometime soon! I pored over the file adding details to my own case's timeline. I now had new suspicions but needed confirmation from Patti. She really was the genius at this sort of thing. Patti helped me on at least half my cases, if not more.

I often joked that thanks to her knowledge and guidance, the guys thought I was a real profiler. She had a large hand in most of my promotions and I counted on her perspective to help me improve.

That weekend we were relaxing on Friday by the pool and just chatting about the week and how it had gone for each of us. I always enjoyed Fridays like this, we could connect and share what happened and usually end up naked somewhere inside or outside the house. We were headed over to Jon and Kathy's for a party Saturday so we both liked these quiet times together before one of those bashes. The parties were fun, and we always said we were going to leave early. In almost every case we stayed far longer because we just couldn't bring ourselves to leave.

As we finished our first bottle and I got up to grab another I looked back at Patti and asked if I could show her a file? She smiled and said, "what Friday would be complete without that?" I returned with the file and poured us each a glass of an excellent Malbec we both enjoyed.

I always thought we should buy more California wines, but we seemed to gravitate to Chilean and Argentinian reds and French whites. Before I gave her the file, I warned her this one was grisly but said I thought it might be connected to my active case. She laughed and said we had both seen just about everything and asked what I thought could possibly throw her off.

I handed her the file and she opened it going through page by page. She looked at me and said she could see why I thought this one was extra gruesome. She held up the first photo I had seen and said, "you definitely have a woman serial killer on your hands." Just like that, calmly and decisively.

I asked what made her so sure and she said that in virtually 100% of cases there was no way a man would cut off another man's junk. It just hits too close to home no matter how screwed up these guys are. They could shoot another guy there, kick him in the groin, maybe even stab him there but cutting it off just did not happen.

Oddly, there seemed to be lines drawn in the sand for even the most depraved among us. Nope, I was looking for a female she said.

I said I agreed with her assessment and told her I was now going to review the other three murders more closely. I needed to determine if there was anything to connect the other homicides other than another dead abuser of a battered woman. Patti mentioned how this change could have been brought about by direct circumstances or some other event in the unsub's life. That was the guess-work part of what she did. We closed the file and watched the sun set as I brought my wife closer to me.

She looked great in this bathing suit; it was one of my favorites. It was a one piece but had holes all over it. It was like the type of thing you might see in a James Bond movie. We quickly forgot about the case and the photos and in short order were enjoying each other by the pool. I wished I could be with her like this all day every day but we both had busy lives at work. I think that was one of the very things that made these times so special. We could just block out the entire world and be happily consumed completely by the other person.

I awoke early on Saturday and was soon in my study reviewing files. I found that I could really focus in there and always made headway on tough cases. I pored over the details in each of the four murders. I had a white board with a combination of notes and sticky notes all over it. I had two large screens for my PC to help me check details and facts and search the internet.

The connection seemed to be the surgical precision of the kills and the fact the women were all being abused by the guy who had been killed. Was this, by any chance, a law enforcement officer? I had certainly seen cases where I thought I might be capable of some of this, but I never actually contemplated doing anything. Law enforcement people had broken the law before, perhaps that was the case here?

The infamous Golden State Killer was in law enforcement.

He was recently arrested thanks to new methods of DNA testing including techniques that had not previously existed. The crime lab was able to test some DNA from DeAngelo's home that directly tied him to some of the murders. They sent his DNA to one of those sites where people send their own samples in to track their lineage and that was where the connection was made. Big brother...

DNA techniques, crime labs and profilers have made a huge amount of progress in the last ten or fifteen years. DeAngelo had gone undiscovered for more than forty years. It wasn't until the FBI renewed their investigation in 2016 that things heated up in one of the most notorious cold cases there has ever been. The DNA information discovered by the lab enabled police to connect many, many outstanding cases with all evidence pointing directly toward DeAngelo.

He is now accused of killing at least twelve people, raping fifty more and robbing hundreds. The twist was that this killer spent SIX YEARS working in law enforcement as a police officer in California.

He was fired in 1979 when he was caught shoplifting a can of dog repellent and a hammer from a local drugstore.

Based on the timeline, he was likely killing people while still employed as a Police Officer. Obviously, that had to be considered here.

What made it likely was that my killer appeared to be dispensing justice in his or her own sick way. The death penalty in California had been abolished long ago but this perp chose to repeal that decision, at least on a personal level.

California has not executed a criminal since 2006. That was when Clarence Ray Allen, 76 years old, legally blind, diabetic and in a wheelchair was put to death at San Quentin. He was already serving a sentence for murder when he organized the killing of three more people.

Allen's case was the basis of the death penalty in California being struck down as "cruel and unusual punishment". Even without a death penalty in place, criminals have continued to be sentenced to death. There are currently more than 740 California inmates on death row. Many have been there for years and years, exhausting every possibility their life might be spared.

A recent election in California included Proposition 66, sponsored by prosecutors. Proposition sixty-six could mean quicker reviews of cases and the return of the death penalty. In California, it currently averages 25 years to complete the appeals process for death row inmates. Prop sixty-six would require the entire appeals process to be completed in five years at most.

At barely more than 50% support for the death penalty, the fight will likely not end soon. This criminal certainly saw his own efforts as being righteous.

I knew there were police officers who were capable of such things and the arrest of DeAngelo helped to drive that point home. Most all of them controlled those urges though. Sure, the odd time one might beat a perp within an inch of his life but that was happening less and less these days.

There were too many dash cams, body cams and cellphones to take crazy chances for a little personal satisfaction. I suppose that in itself could drive someone to go underground and take it to the next level.

In law enforcement, watching all your arduous work be flushed due to a technicality or a smooth-talking defense attorney was very frustrating.

The more facts I reviewed, the tougher I thought it was going to be to catch this killer. Each time I saw a woman riding a motorcycle I found myself wondering if she had the skill, talent and craziness to do what this woman was doing? I finally put the files away and relaxed a bit before we went over to Kathy and Jon's. It always took me a while to clear my head during cases like this, not that I was ever able to completely do so.

Patti threw on a cover up over her holey bathing suit and I just had on some board shorts and a Hawaiian shirt. Patti always looked great. I never minded seeing guys check out my wife. I knew she was hot, and I figured I had married up, but I also knew she was 100% with me. It was a good feeling to have, and we were as close as any couple I had ever known.

We walked up the beach hand in hand to Jonathon and Kathy's. As we stepped up onto the patio their friend Megan was there again. I had noticed last time how attractive she was but hadn't really taken in the whole picture.

She was an awesome physical specimen and just reeked of power. We all started chatting and I asked what she did that she was in such great shape. She explained that she had been a div one athlete in college and had just kept up the training because she enjoyed it so much.

She loved to push herself and break barriers. I couldn't put my finger on it but there seemed to be more to her than met the eye. It was just a feeling I sometimes got, due in no small part to how much Patti had taught me over the years.

She smiled and said, "it looks like you and Patti work out quite a bit yourselves." We said it was the nature of our jobs and just left it at that. It was another fun day. Everyone was in and out of the ocean and the pool and there were just enough people to make it interesting.

More than once, I found myself catching a glimpse of Meg. It seemed each time I looked at her she was just a little more captivating. She had the good looks and high cheekbones that frequently come from a white-Mexican parentage along with the olive-colored skin. You could tell that makeup was only an option for this woman and not required. Then there was her physical condition. If I were a woman, I would certainly want to be in the shape she was in. What am I saying? I would love to be at her level of physical conditioning myself.

Look, I loved my wife deeply, but Meg's long legs, hard stomach and perfect rear end were impossible not to notice. I wished my own shoulders looked as powerful as hers did!

Lastly there was that feeling of confidence that oozed from every pore of her beautiful body. It wasn't the confidence brought on by mere beauty or her obvious physicality but more of an internal strength it seemed. The detective in me was telling himself there really was a lot more to her. I also sensed I would never find out what that was.

But then again, I seemed to always be thinking things like that. Hazard of the profession, I think. I never understood how Patti could turn off her profiling skills either. She was somehow able to block out the things she had seen and the people she had dealt with, a talent I had never acquired.

My worry was that somehow, even though I am madly in love with my wife, this woman had captivated me. When we ran into each other at Luke and Angela's or Kathy and Jon's, I found myself wondering what was she like? What had she done the night before?

What would it be like to be with her? I chalked it up as basic, guys-are-idiots stuff and left it at that.

Nevertheless, it was extremely difficult NOT to look at Meg. Whether she was standing still or moving, you could see her sinewy muscles as they flexed beneath her smooth skin. It appeared she was always ready to pounce. I had honestly never seen anyone in such tip-top physical condition up close.

It was easy to imagine her taking out most any of the cops I knew too. It didn't appear to me she would have any problem whatsoever defending herself in almost any situation.

I found myself imagining what an agent she would make. The two of us working closely, as Patti and I have. She would clearly be a formidable partner.

Chapter Nineteen – Just One More

It had now been a full three weeks since the Palm Springs – El Monte deal and I was feeling the urge to save another woman. I had a rock-solid alibi in place and had displayed a new MO. I knew there was no forensic evidence that could link me. Now that I had seen good old Detective Sharpe and his lovely wife a couple more times, I was sure they had no leads to speak of either. I was feeling confident, and I knew that DNA was the most critical clue to not leave behind.

If it caught up with the Golden State Killer after forty years, it could easily catch up with me too. I went to great lengths to ensure there was no way my DNA could be found related to any crime scenes. It was also critical because, thanks to my former employer, I knew my full DNA profile was in a database somewhere. It was not like I could hide from that.

The authorities would not have to use some side door to skirt the constitution by going to a genealogy site. They would just have to run the DNA from a crime scene as they always did and mine would pop up as a match. You never considered the loss of privacy when you provided your DNA or fingerprints to one agency or another. I sure considered it now.

Nevertheless, it was time to plan another outing. I knew it shouldn't be too close to home and going back to Arizona wasn't the best plan. Before I could take out Bobby safely, I felt I had to do one more in California.

I decided on Oakland. I had now taken out a white guy and three Latinos.

There was no racial profiling or anything, that was just the way cookie crumbled for those guys. Finding a black guy to add to the mix was a clever idea. I didn't want to display a "type" that might help a profiler. Besides, I was sure that was one trait that cut across all racial and socio-economic barriers. I wanted every male regardless of race, creed, color or national origin, to know that abusing women is not acceptable.

I thought Oakland would be a good hunting ground and it was only a quick 370 mile blast up the I-5 if I chose to take the freeway. I used the next weekend at Kathy and Jonathon's to set it up. They had a Friday afternoon bash and I convinced them and a couple of others I was coming down with something.

Bobby and his new girl were there too so I made sure to say hello and make nice with both. I said how great it was to see him and what a lovely couple they made. Inside, of course, I wanted to ask her if he had hit her yet, but I knew that would be a huge mistake. I always watched the two of them closely in hopes of picking up some signs of abuse or the controlling behaviour that typically preceded abuse.

It was time to step up my plan. I was talking to Kathy and excused myself to use the washroom. I spent a little too much time in there and then told Kathy I was feeling sick, and I was going to head home.

I told her I would phone her in the morning when I woke up to check in.

I went home, packed and loaded up and jumped on the Honda to head to Oakland. I had left early enough that I got checked into my second fleabag motel only a little after eight. It was eerily similar to the dump in Phoenix.

I found some humour in the fact that there was consistency amongst these crappy motels. All those expensive chains trying to recreate the same customer experience in the same settings and these joints already had a lock on it. Same crunchy carpets, same stench, same moldy tiles in the bathroom...same everything it seemed.

I got changed into my usual clothes and had another home made garotte in my inside jacket pocket. I also had my voice changer tucked into the inside pocket of my jacket. This would be my first time using the garotte in forever and I was oddly excited. It was such a simple and effective weapon. The garotte was clean, quick and compact. In my other pocket I had two nitrile gloves and a pair of the leather ones.

I had a different plan this time. I wanted it to be clear why this was happening. I wanted word to get out. I wanted to scare as many men as possible into no longer putting their hands on or abusing women. This meant there had to be a witness, someone who would communicate the message I would leave with her as I choked the life out of her abuser.

Even with all the murders in California I wanted this message to be seen and seen often on televisions across the country.

I was dressed in my usual ball cap and blond hair, larger clothes and my glasses. A little makeup applied correctly and there was no way even an eyewitness would identify me. I would also use the balaclava to disguise the fact I was female.

Around ten I headed a few blocks down to a bar I had spotted that looked like a good place to find the right couple. It still amazed me how easy and often one could find a man misbehaving with a woman. I checked for cameras, surveyed the parking lot and headed in to find my desired dark corner of the bar. I sat down and plunked down a five on the dark, sticky table for my Budweiser, telling her to keep the change. I sat and waited and watched. It appeared I would have a few options to choose from.

One couple became much more likely as the night wore on.

He hadn't hit her yet, but I could hear the way he spoke to her, and I could see on her face how trapped she felt. They got up to leave and I followed soon after. They got into a car but before I turned away, I noticed they were not leaving. They smoked either a joint or some hash or crack and then I saw him force her head into his lap. He was clearly holding her there. What the hell was wrong with this type of guy?

Amazingly enough, they went back into the bar together when she was done! I couldn't understand how any woman could stay with a man like that. I altered my thoughts a bit when I recalled that I didn't exactly leave Bobby right away either. Who was I to judge these women?

I was simply here to pass judgement on their abusive men and yet even I was looking for ways to blame the woman. Being judge, jury and executioner was a lot of hats to wear at the same time, but I seemed well-suited for it. I decided I would watch them briefly to confirm and then go lay in wait in the vehicle. The light was burnt out in that part of the parking lot, the remaining ones casting a pall over this section.

It was easy to hide in the back seat, behind the driver. I splashed on a little men's cologne, pulled on my balaclava and got in and waited. It was so hot that I was about to give up when I finally heard the doors of the bar slam open again.

Shortly after that the car door opened, and I felt her plop hard into the seat. I assumed he had thrown her in and was now going around to his door. He got in and said her last effort was only okay. She had better improve when they got home, or she would be in deep trouble.

I chuckled silently to myself thinking he had NO idea how much trouble he was in. I could hear her crying in the seat. I saw and heard nobody else around. I knew I had to act before he started the car. We did not need a car crash to draw attention to us. That was the only drawback to using the garotte, sometimes the victim would thrash around quite a bit.

I felt him fall back into the seat and could see his head against the headrest. I quickly got the wire around his neck and pulled hard. He couldn't make a sound except a gurgling noise as I choked the life out of his worthless body. I looked through the eye holes of my mask at the girl and told her to shut up or she was next. She just watched as the wire started to cut through his skin and he struggled for a breath I knew he would never get.

She watched him as calmly as if she were watching a movie in the comfort of her own home. All that was missing was a big bowl of popcorn. It was an odd reaction to watching someone die right in front of their eyes. I knew she would be no trouble to me.

In a minute or two his lifeless body slumped, and I removed the garotte, replacing it with a zip tie just in case. I pulled the tie as tight as I could and leaned him back in the seat.

I looked the scared, soundless woman in the eyes and told her he would have killed her. I used my voice bender to disguise my voice, so she had no reason to think I was not a male. I told her to understand she had worth, and she should pick better next time. Once someone hits you, they will do it again and again. They never stopped. I told her to tell her story to anyone who would listen. We needed men to understand that there could be consequences to bad behavior. She smiled at me and nodded her head. I knew her life must have been a living hell as the sense of relief from her was palpable.

I got out of the car, went into the alley and ran straight to my hotel, keeping everything with me. I slipped into my room unnoticed, got everything I was wearing into a bag and had it all done in about fifteen minutes. I was now ready for another bonfire somewhere between Oakland and LA. It wasn't too late yet and I figured it might be wise to head out right away.

I filled the coffee maker only half-way, so it would appear I had a cup in the morning. I trashed one of the cups after swirling some grounds in it and dumped a packet of sugar and packet of whitener into the toilet, throwing the empty packages into the trash next to the coffee maker.

I got everything together and slipped out, leaving the do not disturb sign on the door and the two key cards on the table.Even if she did call the cops right away, they had no idea I was on a motorcycle. Also, they would be looking for a larger man with blond hair. The wig was stashed in my luggage and the balaclava was in the burn bag, so I would be fine. Even the garotte was wrapped up in there.

I thought it might make sense to try to get to either Bakersfield or maybe even San Luis Obispo. I could find a quiet place to call Kathy, cough into the burner phone a few times during the call and tell her I would see her in a couple of days.

Nobody had land lines anymore so that made my charade easier to pull off. There was always possible tracking via cell towers, but I had more than one burner phone, so I had no concerns about being tracked. I decided on San Luis as it was only a couple hundred miles down the road. I knew it would be about 2 ½ hours or so to home from there and if I left early there should be no problems.

I rolled into San Luis a little after midnight and scouted for a hotel. I pulled into a Motel Six on Highway 1 just short of town. I knew they were low end, and I figured the chances of a crackhead running the front desk were rather good. I parked out back and donned my blond wig and a ball cap.

I went in and was pleased to see the clerk, as expected, was an obviously hard-core addict complete with needle tracks. I paid with cash, got my keys and headed to the room. There was no chance he would remember me as he seemed totally out of it, his eyes glazed over from what I was sure was constant drug use.

I had a decent sleep and was up and gone early, right after I phoned Kathy. I wanted to do it from the quiet of the room with the TV on. I told her I was still sick and was just going to hole up at home and try to sleep it off. I didn't need anyone at my house ringing the bell and figuring out I wasn't home. I told her I would call when I was feeling better.

It was a nice ride down the coast as the sun came up and reflected off the water as I rode South. The closer I got to home the more nervous I became but it seemed I rolled into my garage unseen. I guess that was the benefit of the quiet hum of a Honda versus the noisy torque of a Harley!

I got in, got all washed up and just watched a couple of movies and kicked back. It was unlikely a murder in Oakland would get any airplay around LA. We had our own murders to worry about, so I wasn't too surprised when I didn't see anything on the news right away. I scanned a few stations including Channel Five Oakland and heard nothing. It would most likely show up in tomorrow's news.

There was nothing until the next evening when I tuned back in. The local news in Oakland was reporting on this murder and the woman's face suddenly filled the shot. She was saying how this guy in a mask saved her life. She shared some of the things I had told her and how easily I had killed her six-foot-three, football player boyfriend. She said I strangled the life out of him and then took the time to tell her not to put up with abusive men. I guessed the word was going to get out now.

The story was picked up by a few stations and by the next day I assumed it had been seen just about everywhere. I knew Special Agent Sharpe would now be getting the details. I just wished he would say something about this case at one of Kathy's parties! Anything to give me a clue as to what they had. I would think that law enforcement would start directing more resources toward apprehending this serial killer. If I could be any more careful, I would need to be.

I smiled when I learned I now had an official serial-killer name...The Angel of Death. Hmm, I had never thought of myself as an angel, or a serial killer, but it did have a nice ring to it.

I was looking forward to the next party at Jonathon and Kathy's and really hoping Colin Sharpe might open up about his (our) case. I really wanted to find out where they were at before taking out my final, and original, target.

I knew for certain there was almost no forensics, and I didn't see how they could possibly have a lead, but you never really know for certain. My military experience taught me that it was always the trivial details that closed difficult cases. I also knew that paying attention to details the way that I did there would be precious few crumbs on which to build a case.

In most complex cases where the killer was caught there was always one slip-up that got them started. Once that slip-up was made and the police got the tiniest of clues, they would often refocus their efforts.

It was always easier for them to find actual evidence with a new perspective. It was at that point where even the minutest detail could be picked up. Although they were getting better overall, various agencies of law enforcement were far worse at solving homicides now than in the past. At least I had that fact on my side.

In 1965 law enforcement cleared slightly more than 90% of the homicides being committed in the USA. If we fast-forward to 2012 that clearance rate was down to 64%. That means one third of all homicides being committed are not being solved! It appeared that either law enforcement was overwhelmed or that criminals were getting better at covering their tracks. I supposed there was also a larger volume to be considered as well.

In hard numbers, since 1980, there remains over 210,000 unsolved homicides in the United States.

With performance like that, I firmly believed the chances of them catching little ole me were very slim indeed. The average criminal had nothing on me and a third of those were getting away with murder.

I knew they had no answer for my skillset and talent for doing what I was doing. I was also driven by a desire that was righteous, saving women by eliminating the worst men. The very people the courts seemed so bad at stopping.

Sure, it was up to law enforcement professionals to gather all the evidence and build the cases for the prosecutors but too often there were holes. Holes those lawyers and criminals could use to their advantage.

Slick haired defense lawyers frequently seemed to have the upper hand and I had no idea how they could do it. When all the evidence indicates someone was guilty and you secure a verdict of innocent from a somewhat gullible jury how do you live with yourself? They were nothing more than super smooth-talking, very highly paid, salesmen in my eyes.

Their clients many times tell their defense attorney they DID do it, and they STILL get them off. Once that fact was revealed to their lawyer it became privileged information. The lawyer could neither discuss nor disclose the conversation. Sure, there were some ways around that, but few lawyers would risk the loss of their lucrative career if caught.

I understand there needs to be checks and balances in our justice system but too often it seems completely broken. I wasn't delusional or anything. I gathered my own evidence, saw with my own eyes what was happening and sentenced the perpetrators to death. Now that is justice!

Frontier justice maybe, but justice nevertheless, at least in my eyes and the eyes of the women I had saved so far. I knew for a fact that each of their lives were better now than before.

Chapter Twenty – Back at Kathy and Jonathon's

It was a couple of weeks after that when there was another party, finally! Okay, it wasn't really that long but it seemed like forever. I was eager to try and find out information. We were all hanging around in the ocean or the pool when up walks Colin. He was looking solid as usual, I smiled and said hello. I looked around and asked where Patti was. He said she was home sick, but she forced him to come to the party anyway. I grinned in response to his slight grimace and said, "I'm stag too, why don't you grab a drink and come keep me company?"

I couldn't come right out and ask, but I hoped with enough open doors he might share something about the case. We were just chatting about nothing in particular when I said he looked a little tired and asked if everything was okay. He said this case was really getting to him and he wasn't sure if everything connected or not. Finally, he came out and asked if I had seen anything on the news about the guy, they were calling the Angel of Death. I almost asked him why he thought it was a guy but quickly caught myself. There was absolutely nothing to be gained, and perhaps much to lose, by making such a stupid comment.

I told him I had seen something about that. This angel of death cut off some guy's junk or something.

He had a pained look on his face, and I laughed and said, "right, you guys are really connected with those things eh?" He smiled and said he preferred his attached.

I laughed again and said Patti probably does too and just left it at that.

I excused myself to use the washroom and I noticed in the reflection off the glass that his eyes followed me all the way. Interesting but not crazy, guys liked to look at my butt. I supposed special agents weren't all that special after all, they were just regular guys. Most of them dogs.

As I came out of the house and walked back towards him, he was eyeing me up and down again. This time I could see his face clearly and I had seen that look before. Hungry, but trying to hide it. Attached but perhaps wishing he weren't. There was no way I was going near a married guy and my resolve was even stronger because I knew Patti. I just figured it was that whole concept of getting your appetite anywhere, as long as you ate at home. It still made me a little uncomfortable though. After all, although we weren't lifelong buddies or anything, we were all friends.

Bobby and his girlfriend showed up and they came over to say hi on their way to the sand. I was congenial and commented on how great his girlfriend looked in her bathing suit. "Is that a new one?" I asked. She smiled and said Bobby got it for her. I kept to myself the fact that I had one similar that I knew I would now never wear again.

It figured that Bobby was one of those guys who tried to make a current girlfriend look like one who had gotten away.

Sort of like John Derek. His third wife, Linda Evans resembled a younger version of second wife Ursula Andress and fourth wife, Bo Derek, was the spitting image of Linda Evans when she was young. He just got in the habit of upgrading to a new model whenever the current one was getting old, but he wanted someone who looked similar. I sensed Bobby might behave in the same way if he could afford it.

It was a fun day to be sure, but Colin never shared any more details of his case. I knew I could not probe or be the one to bring it up and even if he did again, I had to conceal my interest. I stayed a little longer with him before excusing myself to circulate. I met a few more people and then sat with Kathy and Angela for a bit.

I told them that I thought Bobby had hit the jackpot with this girl. I shared with them how she was so pretty, and they seemed to be a good fit for each other. To anyone who knew us and knew we dated it was plainly obvious that I was happy for him. I loved that I had the ability to fool anybody whenever I wanted. I could beat any lie detector test and its operator. I had been very well trained in all these areas and I was going to use it to my advantage. It amazed me what you could be taught and that the capacity to learn can keep increasing.

To be honest though, she was your almost-too-cute California blond with a beach body. She was clearly no rocket scientist, but I don't think that is what guys like Bobby want anyway. They don't usually hang around Cal-Tech looking for potential trophy wives. Not that there weren't a bunch of attractive women at that school. Those women were not weak enough to be fooled by a guy like Bobby and if they did get caught up with him, they would run at one sniff of his controlling behaviour.

If you were a woman at Cal-Tech you were top of the heap in the brains department and usually quite able to take care of yourself. Guys like Bobby wanted to find someone where they sensed a weakness that they can prey on. Whether it was lack of intelligence, low self-esteem or daddy issues, they were able to spot those traits. They then use that weakness to control these women. It can be anything and men like him have a real knack for finding those people. They were profilers in a way, amateur ones, but profilers, nevertheless.

When the psychological and emotional control starts to weaken or doesn't feed their ego enough is when they start the physical stuff. In the worst cases it escalates to severe beatings and even death and those are the very people I wanted to find.

Their biggest weakness, after their own ego, was their need to dominate and abuse women and I used that against them. Rage and anger always clouded a person's judgement, so these guys typically were not smart enough to hide forever. Sure, there were some who were surprisingly good, but I could root them out too. It just took a little longer to find them.

Once found, I would exact the revenge these women could not and that truly made me happy.

Chapter Twenty 1 – I May Have to Stay Away

It had been a long week for me. The department was under pressure to clear cases, and I was starting to hear it from my superiors. Whenever the media created a name for a serial killer, the internal pressure to close that case ramps up a few extra notches. Public pressure increases, and the media are like a school of sharks when the waters are chummed with pieces of a hot story.

Crap runs downhill, and my boss's boss likely raked him over the coals as did his boss's boss and so on up the food chain. Like a sewer pipe, it started out small but each successive level the pipe diameter increases. Each boss had to add his own spin. By the time it gets to guys like me, what started out as a pen sized pipe was now a 36-inch sewer main.

I normally did not respond, nor was I usually affected by that pressure, but this one was a little different. I hadn't really wrapped up a significant case for a couple of years now. At fifteen years in I was starting to be concerned as to whether I had lost my edge or, worse yet, the higher ups were losing confidence in me.

It was a challenge every law enforcement officer may face in his or her career.

In the FBI and CIA though these situations were much more difficult. More people at risk and more murders in the papers were never a good thing. Of course, the CIA mostly operated outside of the continental US and the FBI handled everything inside, so the pressure was always greater on us.

Oh well, this was my lot in life. I KNEW I was good at my job but never had I worked a case with so little hard evidence to go on. There were so few clues being discovered I thought this person had to be a well-trained professional.

It had been a difficult week and when Patti mentioned that Kathy and Jonathon were having a bash this weekend, I found myself looking forward to it. I was ready to unwind, have a few drinks and have a few laughs. As the time to leave approached, Patti said she was feeling terrible. I said no problem I would stay home and take care of her. She told me there was really nothing to do. She was going to take a couple of sleeping pills and hopefully wake up refreshed. She made me promise her I would go to the party without her and have a good time. She was always very aware when I needed to cut loose a bit. She usually knew it before I did. Those profiling skills of hers weren't always a blessing.

Against my will, I wandered up the beach to Jonathon and Kathy's place. As I walked the short distance, seeing a couple of women in bikinis splashing around, thoughts of Meg entered my head. I kept thinking about her riding a Harley and her obvious strength.

I tried to convince myself it was case related, but I knew it was not. I tried to scrub those thoughts out of my mind, recalling last weekend on the patio with my wife. That helped.

I turned onto the stairs and was greeted by Jonathon handing me a cold beer. He saw me coming up the beach and had one ready for me.

What a great neighbor! We stood on the stairs for a while drinking our beers and chatting about life as we watched the waves gently roll in and settle slowly onto the sand. Each one ending in a thin line of whitish foam only to be dragged back out to the surf, the riptides far too powerful for the remnants of a wave to fight against.

Jonathon was always good to speak with, especially about investments. I had made some good money thanks to his advice, and I always kept an open ear when he started talking about the markets.

I went up onto the main patio and saw a few people and sure enough, there was Megan Hernandez. I tried to keep moving but she spotted me, said hello, and asked where Patti was. I told her she was home sick. Meg suggested I grab a fresh drink and come keep her company for a while. Geez, this might be harder than I thought! I grabbed a beer for each of us and headed back to the chairs.

Unlike my usual self, I mentioned the case generally and told her how it was really a tough one. I brushed over a few very high-level details and that was about it. I don't typically discuss cases with anyone but Patti or my co-workers because possibly giving away a key detail is far too big a risk. You just never really know who you are talking to, so I have found it safer to just keep quiet.

I was wondering if I had talked a bit about my case in a feeble attempt to impress Meg? We sat and chatted about not much at all. She excused herself to use the washroom in the house and I could not take my eyes off her as she walked away. She was certainly a powerful athlete. She was every bit as great looking from the back as from the front too. I just watched her beautiful rear end on top of those gorgeous, powerful legs as she walked into the house.

I had my feet up and was really relaxing when I caught her coming back out of the house in the corner of my eye. Seeing her walk towards me was even more challenging. It was so difficult to appear to not be looking at her when I was so intent on seeing as much as I could. She moved with a grace that belied her overall height and musculature.

There HAD to be something in her past. I didn't think I should find out what that was either as it had the potential to make her even more desirable. I started to think this was some sort of test.

I remembered she had lived with our other neighbor Bobby for a brief time, but it didn't last. Of course, it didn't.

Not much seemed to last with Bobby. When it came to women, he had the attention span of a gnat. I did find it quite hard to understand what he could possibly find wrong with Meg though? Maybe she was just too much woman for him? I got the impression she could be too much woman for most men.

I thought it unlikely, but she might even be a real ball-buster as they say. Perhaps a bit of a well disguised man-hater.

I think most guys don't like that but what attracted me to Patti was her self- sufficiency, her confidence and her mind. She was also mentally tough. Yes, she was all those things, and an attractive and sensual woman.

Patti really was the complete package, which made my attraction (perhaps interest?) to Meg even less understandable. What was wrong with us guys? We could have the best gig in the world and somehow, we can think maybe the grass is greener elsewhere.

I knew I would have to forget this, but I also knew that it would be difficult to do so. I didn't stay too much longer as I wanted to get home and check on Patti, now that I was thinking about her.

I made the rounds and said good-bye to Kathy and Jon last and then took off up the beach.

Chapter Twenty 2 – Bobby or Not?

With all the groundwork in place it was now time to formulate a plan to take out Bobby. I also knew it was the right thing to do when I saw his girlfriend in the washroom at a party. She didn't see me, but I saw her touching up her makeup around her eye and it looked like she had been hit. I wanted to ask her directly but could not risk letting on that I knew something.

I wasn't sure, but as I watched her and Bobby at the last gathering, I could see the subtle control coming out. Just the way he took her arm and led her a certain way this or that. I watched as he quickly inserted himself into a conversation, even if she was having it with a male and female and not just a male. He was exhibiting all the behaviours of an abuser. No surprise there, it is very difficult to hide your true self for any length of time.

I knew it was time. I needed to make him suffer and I wanted him to know it was me, but I also wanted it to look like it fit the Angel of Death pattern. In addition, I felt I needed to get them focused on this Angel of Death being a man. I knew I would have to beat him badly before releasing him from this earth and saving his current girlfriend. I thought about a robbery gone bad type scenario, but I wanted it known that he was an abuser, just like the other ones.

I ran, I worked out during the day and in the evenings, I planned. I watched his schedule as closely as I could without arousing suspicion. I had an untraceable link to his wireless network and was able to monitor things like emails, schedules and everything online, so that helped.

When I left active duty, I had a few toys and devices that I thought might come in handy some time, so I took them with me. Here they were, coming in very handy.

I was able to get a good handle on when he worked, when he worked late and his favorite girlfriend times. I knew he liked to have alone-time too and I was able to ascertain how often and how long that happened. Thanks to a transparent view of his banking records and credit cards I knew that on payday he usually liked to hit a strip bar or two. Typical.

I watched and watched and kept all my notes on paper. The monitoring was done with an untraceable bit of software anyway but even if they did somehow trace it successfully, they would find it tracked to a cheap laptop in Russia. It was so easy to create a false digital footprint these days, no wonder elections can be tampered with.

The FBI simply did not have intelligence to equal what I had learned. Some of their tools were much less effective than what I had because mine were designed to elude exactly what the FBI, CIA and other agencies used.

Part of being able to track, monitor and avoid foreign countries intelligence meant that, by default, you could usually avoid ours as well.

That was one of the reasons all my notes, plans, drawings and ideas were kept on paper. Paper that I could easily burn that would be destroyed forever. I found it humorous that in the digital age the best way to keep things secret now was to use good old paper and a pencil!

Those forensics folks could recover data from hard drives with ease. I have seen some that were burned, sledgehammered or hammered AND burned and they still got information. It seemed no matter what you did to those things it was impossible to ever erase completely anything.

Paper, on the other hand, had again become the perfect medium. Write down all kinds of information, draw up all sorts of plans and all you had to do was shred and then burn. Gone forever, nothing recoverable, secrets committed to an ashy grave.

It would be much the same with the elimination of Bobby. It would be done the old-fashioned way, a serious kick-ass beatdown that I would enjoy completely. I knew how quickly and efficiently I could kill a man, but I vowed this one would take time.

I had a good handle on the how and the why was clearly obvious. Now I had to figure out the where and the when part of the deal. That required a great deal more thought and planning.

I considered making it look like a robbery on the beach. I decided that would make it too difficult for people to make the connection to him being an abuser. Local police officers would think it was just a robbery gone bad. I wouldn't have enough time to beat him, and it would be far too easy to get caught. Besides, I had no desire to kill him quickly. I needed time and privacy to do what I had to do.

One of the more successful methods of luring a male was to use his own ego against him. Even the nastiest looking guy did not think it out of the ordinary when a good-looking woman hit on him.

At least the ones who thought like Bobby and the rest of his kind would not wonder why. After all they viewed themselves as quite the catch for any woman. Most were complete narcissists with a little misogyny thrown in.

I determined the best option would be to approach him after the strip club. I would accidentally bump into him and convince him that I missed him. His guard would be down, he will have had a few drinks. All the blood would be flowing away from the big head too.

It would be easy to convince him I want him again. My plan was coming together but the riskiest part of it was yet to be finalized.

I had thought about many places but decided, even though it was the most dangerous, to take him back to his own house. The place where he first struck me. I always liked a little bit of irony and knew I would love the look on his face when he realized what was really happening. I imagined the resignation and fear in his eyes when he finally understood that I wanted him all right, I wanted him dead!

As I tracked his activity, I noticed he frequented one strip bar more than the others. Typical I suppose, guys seemed to always think that with enough visits there was always a chance they might be able to take their favorite girl home. I don't think it ever happened, but they seemed to always have hope that it would. If they just bought enough dances and made her see he was "one of the good ones".

They were too dense to realize that it was all about her making money from him and they were never going to meet outside the club. This club was far removed from where he lived but reasonably close to his office. I had confirmed his girlfriend was away for the week, so I had no worries anyone would be at his house. I waited for his next payday, and it was time to put my plan into action.

I selected a skimpy top and a nice skirt that I knew would ride up when I sat down. I needed to make sure to keep his interest until I got him safely into his house. I skipped the bra too just to be extra-positive the big brain couldn't take over control of his weak body.

For these reasons, I had always found men the easiest to kill. So many of them were just a walking bag of hormones. It was laughable how you could lead them around by the nose so easily! Even the most disgusting and ugliest of men seemed to have no trouble believing an attractive woman would want him. It was a serious character flaw in most males that was so easy to exploit.

I was all dressed and ready. Tight leather gloves in my purse along with one or two "aids" and it would soon be time. I contemplated the previous four men whom I had helped slip the surly bonds of this earth. "The surly bonds of earth", I recall I was only six years old when I first heard that.

It was Ronald Reagan soon after the Challenger disaster. He paraphrased John Gillespie Magee, Jr when he said, "We will never forget them, nor the last time we saw them – this morning, as they prepared for their journey, and waved good-bye, and slipped the surly bonds of earth to touch the face of God."

The guys I was taking out would never touch the face of God. They would never even come close. Instead, they would stare for eternity into the red eyes of Lucifer. Flames licking at their feet as they endured their punishment, whatever that would be.

I determined that while I was doing the right thing and saving women, I was also enjoying this. The last seconds of their lives gave my life more meaning and more purpose. I felt useful again. I hoped I could stop after Bobby, but I just wasn't positive that would be the case now. I was helping so many women, protecting them from beatings or worse. I had seen so much abuse with which I had not yet dealt. I didn't see myself as Supergirl or anything, just someone who had all the tools to get the job done. For me, this was a job that needed to get done.

Payday rolled around, and I tracked his cellphone and could see that he was parked at his favorite strip bar. My surveillance told me he would spend at least two hours there. I left my house around 10:30 PM carrying a small bag with my heels while I wore a pair of runners. I had some nitrile gloves in my purse too, I never leave home without them.

Snatching a car was the best way to avoid detection. Cabs, Uber, public transit all would provide opportunities for people to see me, and I didn't want that.

Quite a few blocks away I located a car that would be easy to grab. It was old enough that it would be simple to steal and new enough it wouldn't break down.

I was into the car and driving quietly away in a couple of minutes. I loved these little Hondas. I thought to myself that I might look at a new one for me but then got back to the task at hand. I drove the car over close to the bar and parked a few blocks away on an out of the way street. No parking signs, no time limits and no parking passes required. It wouldn't be discovered for quite a while.

I got out, removed my gloves and stuck them into my purse. There was no DNA anywhere. No fingerprints, no sweat and no hair. I ensured I was completely void of hair before I left the house. I had even shaved my head. I always liked it when I did that. It made me feel like a real badass.

I slipped off my runners, put on my heels and started walking towards the bar. Geez I hated shoes like this. I had no idea how women could walk in these things all the time. We were coming up on the time I would expect him to be leaving so I would just wander past as slowly as I could. There were larger office buildings close by and the rail line was just on the other side of the street so explaining my presence would be easy. Thankfully I only had to wander past twice. As I was about to turn around, out strolled Bobby, thankfully alone.

I mustered up the sweetest voice I could and looked up at him. "My gawd, bobby how ARE you doing?" He said it was so good to see me and then asked what I was doing in that part of town. I told him I had been on a lousy date downtown and the dirt-bag had stranded me. Internet dating was not all it was cracked up to be. He said how terrible that was and offered to give me a ride home. I thanked him, hugged him close and told him how much I missed him. He smiled and said he missed me too and squeezed me a little tighter.

I looked up at him seductively and asked if we could just go to the beach at his place rather than take me home. I said I didn't want to be alone after this night. I could see the gears turning in his hormone-influenced little brain. He readily agreed, asking me if I wanted to drive.

I said no thanks that we would be better off with him driving. I had my hand on his thigh the whole time we were driving to his house. I was pleased to see there was nobody around at all by the time we rolled up to his garage. I was trying my best to make convincing small talk and thanking him for rescuing me.

We pulled into the garage, and he closed the door quickly behind us leaning over to kiss me at the same time.

I forced myself to appear that I liked his vile mouth on me again and eased my lips apart to complete the ruse. He probed my mouth with his tongue as his filthy hand grazed my breast. Although this was always the easiest way to get a man where I wanted him, it really disgusted me. I knew it would all be over soon however, and I could stomach anything for a brief time.

After all, I had been tortured more than once in my career and was able to detach so I could focus on the task at hand. Those were a couple of the more interesting stories I could never tell anyone in my new life, but I longed to share with my old buddies. I sometimes imagined myself at a party telling a small group about how each time torturers enjoyed extraordinarily little time with the upper hand. I would go on to describe the terrible pain I inflicted on them once I had turned the tables.

They underestimated me because I was a woman, thinking it would be easy to get me to reveal secrets. That was always their weak spot. I laughed on the inside as they attempted to scare me by talking about what they were going to do me. They would soon resort to actual physical punishment but that only served to strengthen my resolve as I contemplated what I would do to them. No talking about it. No warnings. Just decisive and damaging action.

I wanted to tell someone how the first time it had happened I slowly killed each of my captors.

Three men who drastically underestimated who they had captured. Three men who didn't get careless or anything, they just had the wrong person, and had no idea what was coming. They did minor damage to me before I used one of them getting too close to escape my restraints. Now it was my turn!

I would break a limb, ensuring they were compound fractures so that they would bleed. I would break a second limb in a similar manner. Each one careless enough to get just a little bit too close to me, still not realizing who they were dealing with. I let them see each other slowly bleed to death as I sat stoically watching and, at the time, wishing I had a different job. I had no intention of using my L-pill with these bozos and the second time went just about the same. Oh well. These events lived somewhere between PTSD-inducing nightmares and fond memories, depending upon the day on which the thoughts entered my mind.

Back to Bobby and the task at hand. I smiled at him and said, "let's finish this inside big guy, I need you now." He came around and opened my door and helped me out. I had gone to great pains to touch absolutely nothing in the car and was positive that was still the case. I was 100% confident there was no forensic evidence that could place me anywhere close to the scene of this crime.

He led me into the house and as we got through the door he turned, pulled me to him and kissed me again. I was ready to throw up but knew I only had to keep this up for a short while longer and I could get to work.

I told him I was going to freshen up and excused myself, suggesting he get us some wine. I knew his security system was in the closet in that same hallway. I reached in and pulled out the cables and removed the power plug from the socket for good measure. I would take the whole box with me when I left, after completing my task. I went into the washroom, donned my tight leather gloves and walked out with my hands behind my back. When he saw me, he made some stupid comment about handcuffs as he approached.

When he was at the right range, I struck hard with my left hand and caught him right on the button. He went down in a heap as I had knocked him out cold. I drug him to the living room, so I could enjoy the view of the Pacific while I beat him to death. He came around a few minutes later and quickly realized his legs and arms were zip-tied to one of his heavy living room chairs. I had gagged him to ensure there would be little noise to give this away. I wanted to take my time, enjoy myself and really make him pay.

I watched the look in his eyes change to fear as he began to comprehend what was really happening here.

I got the impression he was thinking this was just going to be a beating, so I pulled another chair over and set it right in front of him. I sat down and just stared at him for a little while.

I looked into his soulless eyes and said, "I don't know for sure how many women you have abused and beaten but I know of two for certain. I also know that hitting me was the worst person you could have hit."

I went on to explain what I used to do for a living and how I extracted information from people. I even shared my torture stories with him and explained what I did to each person, in minute detail. I told him that I had killed, without leaving a trace of evidence, more than fifty people. His eyes were getting wide now as he realized that struggle was futile. I knew this would take a while and I knew I would enjoy every second of his pain.

I asked him if he liked to hit women, or did it just happen? Had he been beaten up by a woman or his mother or something even stranger? I asked a whole lot of rhetorical questions simply to watch the fear in his eyes build.

I knew that I could punish someone and inflict enough damage that they would bleed to death internally. It is a very painful way to die, excruciating really. You feel your body is simply going to explode and that is exactly what it is doing, until you finally shut down and simply die. Bobby would soon feel this pain. He would know the feeling of resignation as he slowly died, unable to do anything about his inevitable demise.

I wanted to start with the root cause of his problem. I leaned towards him, so I could listen to the muffled sounds, and drove my fist deep into his groin. Just the one shot as I couldn't have a repeat of the good old Lorena Bobbitt deal. I just wanted him to feel the pain and the hurt and sit with that for a while. Tears came to his eyes quickly and I just laughed at him.

Although he was zip-tied it was done in such a way, using towels and padding that it would not be apparent that he was restrained during the beating. I suppose it didn't really matter anyway; it was just habit on my part.

I circled around behind him and drove my gloved fist hard into his right cheek. I could tell I had knocked out at least one tooth and knew there would be blood, so I loosened the gag to allow him to spit rather than choke. I quickly retied the gag and stepped back. I slapped him hard with the back of my left hand, my knuckles quickly raising a welt on his face. I bent over and leaned toward him as I drove my fist into, and almost right through his rib cage.

He groaned through the gag as the air rushed out of his lungs. The feel of my fist crashing into his skin and his body collapsing inward under my power was something I quite enjoyed.

These methods were typically used to extract information by inflicting the maximum punishment yet still leaving the subject alive. Many times, this was done with the subject blindfolded but there was no need for that here. I needed him to see me each time I struck him. I wanted him to see me smiling as I punished him, genuinely enjoying what I was doing. By watching his eyes closely, I could also accurately gauge his pain level. After all, I wouldn't want him to pass out too soon. I wanted to keep him on the edge for as long as I could.

Getting information was clearly not my goal here. I knew everything about this scumbag that I needed to know. Unlike the others, I was taking a great deal of pleasure in this. Sure, I didn't hate the others, but this was one was very personal. Each blow I struck I imagined it was balancing out the likely hundreds of times he had hit a woman.

The psychological training our country provided me should have left me void of emotion and in the past, it had. This was quite obviously a whole separate set of circumstances. I was invested in this one, heavily. Each blow was a payback for what he had done to me. Each strike generating a warm fuzzy feeling for me and intense pain for him.

Knowing where each internal organ was, I was able to place my blows where the pain would be agonizing, but never enough to cause him to pass out or die.

I had already decided the final blow would come after I untied him. It would be two final blows. The first to obliterate his liver and the next and final one to destroy his spleen. There would already be enough damage to other organs for him to bleed to death internally, but I wanted pain and lots of it.

I kept up my work for another hour and he was already swelling like a bloated body that had been in the water for a couple of days. Thanks to the damage I did to his vocal chords the gag was no longer needed. He could whine quietly but that was about it. He sounded sort of like those Basenji dogs, the ones who can't bark. They just sort of whine.

With the gag removed I stepped back and unleashed a half-power roundhouse kick to the head. My leg snapped out like a whip and connected solidly, surprising him. His head bounced to the side as he gasped loudly. I decided enough was enough. It was time to finish him.

I undid the ties from his legs first and then his arms and helped him to his feet. He was hunched over and in a lot of pain as I spoke to him. I told him he should never have hit women and asked him what the hell was wrong with him. He gave no response of course, he couldn't talk!

He made a feeble attempt to swing at me. I laughed in his face as he could barely lift his weak little arm.

I grew tired of the game and moved in closer, delivering an extremely hard blow that I knew would destroy his liver. I could tell it was perfectly placed as I watched his side quickly swell up and start to turn color from the blood oozing into his body cavity. He doubled over in pain, and I had to lift him back up again.

I propped him up over the counter and I whispered in his ear that the next blow would be even more painful. I told him, on the bright side, this would hasten his demise and bring about the end of his pain. I wished him well in hell, stepped back and exploded his spleen with a devastating shot.

Laila Ali would have been proud of me. Now there was an impressive athlete, taking up boxing at age 18, she ruled the world for her whole career. She only boxed for about seven years, having 24 total fights and retired undefeated. She won twenty-one of those fights by knockout. That apple did not fall far from the tree. She held five titles at the same time during her reign. I even think Muhammad Ali would have been proud too, if my fight had been in a ring and against an opponent who could challenge me.

Bobby fell to the ground, and I sat in the chair and watched his life slowly slip away. He took a little longer to die than I had figured but finally he was gone.

I ensured he was dead and then gathered up what I didn't want to leave behind and put on some new nitrile gloves. I went to the car after grabbing the security hard drive. There was little blood outside of his body and virtually none of it on me. I cleaned off what little there was. I put on my blond wig, baseball hat and clothes I had brought with me.

I hopped in the car, opened the garage door and drove away watching as the door descended slowly behind me. The closing door a metaphor for my own awakening from a nightmare. A solid wall now placed between myself and that bad chapter in my life.

I had parked my own car about fifteen minutes away where it would not be noticed. I drove over close to that area and found another isolated spot to park his car and leave it. I considered burning it but knowing I left no forensic evidence behind, what would be the point in doing that? No sense drawing attention to the situation.

I parked the car and left the keys laying on the road next to the driver's door. It would appear as if someone parked and then dropped their keys. In that neighborhood a car like this wouldn't last long. Some dope would see the keys and drive it away for a joyride or maybe even to a chop shop. Either way, it was going to disappear. There were always criminals coming to the good side of the tracks looking for easy boosts.

I walked a block over to my own car and hopped in. I drove straight home and right into the garage. It was about 2:00 AM or so by then and the street was clear. I took all the clothes I was wearing, the gloves and anything else that had been in his house and bagged them up. There were a few serious incinerators not that far away. I thought I might use one of those if I didn't want a bonfire somewhere. There was no way I could use my own firepit so that was never an option. I would destroy the security system completely sometime in the next few days after extracting and obliterating the hard drive.

I had a long, hot shower and then crawled into bed. My hands were a little sore, even though there were only a few blows to hard flesh. I was protected by the leather gloves, so it wasn't anything I couldn't handle. I slept like a baby waking up around 10:00 in the morning.

I awoke relaxed and ready to face the day. I had a sense of freedom and accomplishment from what I had done. There were no feelings even close to remorse, simply happy feelings.

I decided a run was in order, so I got my gear on, queued up the tunes and headed out. I loved to run. It was so freeing, and I liked the way the endorphins flooded my body as I pushed myself like I had in the old days.

Always farther and faster, sprinting at times to ensure I kept my fitness level high. I enjoyed the way I could still explode and turn on the afterburners, even during a longer run.

I hit the gym the next day and ran into Kathy and Angela who were talking about another party the following weekend. It seemed like that was all they did, but they were fun parties. I gave them a definite maybe and then started really working out. I liked this gym but only kept coming here because it was so well equipped, and my friends were here too. I would prefer a gym with fewer looky-loos to be completely honest.

I got a kick out of how the guys tried to watch me without getting caught. Squats were especially fun as I would load up the bar with eight or ten 45-pound plates and quietly grind out a few sets.

No grunting and groaning or any of that garbage. I loved the sense of accomplishment I got when I pushed my own limits. That is always what drove me, exceeding what I thought I could do.

Most gyms were quite humorous places it seemed to me. Guys were always so loud when they trained. You would think they were lifting a five-ton truck when they were often moving less weight than I was. Only difference was I was doing it quietly.

I relished the sense of calm and control that occupied my mind when I was training. What I now seemed to be unable to control was wondering which one of these dirt-bags abused women? It seemed to be two main types that did it. It was either big, strong men like I saw in the gym or skinny guys. I got re-focused and finished my workout, meeting up with the girls in the locker room before I left.

They again mentioned the party and said it wouldn't be the same without me. I told them to quit bugging me, that I would be there. I added one would have to be an idiot to skip a party where Jon was surely going to try some new recipes. I tried to find out if he was introducing anything new, but they always left that up to him. It was top-secret.

I got home that night and still heard nothing on the news. The next morning, I got a frantic phone call from Kathy. She said there were cops everywhere just up their street. She said she tried to take a look, and they seemed to be focused on Bobby's house. I gave my best surprised voice and asked if she knew what had happened. She told me she didn't and asked if I had heard from him at all. I told her we had broken up like three months ago why would I have heard from him? I asked her to keep me posted and I asked her if the party was still on. She said of course, that was a few days away anyway. I got myself calmed down, thinking maybe the girlfriend had gone over to the house and that was how he was discovered so soon.

Oh well, it was inconsequential how he was found or who found him. He was gone, and the world was now a slightly better place. I had removed another scumbag from the planet, and I felt better because of it. I secretly wished I could stand in front of reporters and tell them why this was happening. Maybe even do it on the steps of the courthouse. Judge Megan has taken another scumbag off the streets, has a nice ring to it. Of course, there aren't any judges who are also executioners any more since the days of the wild west are far behind us.

I felt a little like Joe Arpaio, the fellow who served as Sheriff of Maricopa country in Arizona for twenty-four years. He was always extra tough on criminals and was the guy who had prisoners living in tents and made them wear pink boxers among other "innovative" things. He was always in the news it seemed. I found it humorous that there were huge campaigns against his re-election, but he would win elections with more than 90% of the vote in most cases.

Joe was living proof that people WANTED justice and they preferred criminals to be punished and not coddled. Many simply didn't want their friends knowing they thought that way. It just wasn't de rigueur. It was more draconian than anything, but he had a great deal of success. If not rehabilitating criminals, then by having them help to pay for their own incarceration by growing their own food and working in the community.

Bobby was now gone. My original reason for my rampage had been eliminated. I now had to decide if I was truly finished or not. I thought one more might be the last. Something a little further away, like the Oakland one, might be the best way to ensure my anonymity. I wasn't going to make any hasty decisions. I knew I had more work to do, it was only a question of how much more.

I decided I wouldn't make up my mind until after the party this weekend. Those parties always helped me bring things into focus and decide what I should or should not do. I don't know what kind of sign I was looking for, but I was hoping for something to guide my decision.

I was starting to feel like I HAD to continue and being driven by emotion or dark thoughts is always dangerous. I still cannot describe the things that were going through my head. I could have gotten psychological help or counselling through a separate branch of the VA for people like me but that would be too dangerous. As much as those shrinks are supposed to maintain patient confidentiality, I'm fairly sure when it comes to the military all bets are off.

I had a feeling that senior officers were advised on the down low of anything out of the ordinary.

The risk to me would not be worth the possibility of being helped. When I was serving, I had been sent to see one of those folks once. It seemed no matter what I said he would ask how that made me FEEL. Hells bells, in many cases I didn't really feel anything.

I was satisfied I had completed a task and that was that.

I quickly learned if I wanted these sessions to end, I had to tell him what he was after. That was easy enough to do so I did it. Once completed I vowed I would never again see one of those nutbars. I simply was not convinced that all the talking in the world would make what I had seen go away.

Chapter Twenty 3 – My Next-Door Neighbor Was Killed

I wasn't sure if I felt like going to Jonathon's for a party, but Patti seemed to really want to go. She said she wanted to relax with friends as it wasn't every day there was a murder right next door! I conceded and agreed to go. It really was a complete fallacy that us FBI types were a bunch of boring people.

The day before, I had heard the sirens early in the morning and was shocked when they pulled up right next door and immediately set a perimeter. It was obvious something serious had happened. It looked like a lot more than a robbery. There were too many police for that to be the case.

Normally local police officers are not too happy about having the feds around, but I grabbed my credentials and thought I would try my luck. I decided that I should let them do their thing for a while, so I did not go out immediately. I waited, not so patiently, in the house for a couple of hours, trying to evaluate the situation through our windows.

Finally, I could not wait any longer and I went outside. There were officers everywhere, dogs sniffing around, it was your typical murder scene.

I spotted who I thought was the Officer in Charge and went up to him introducing myself as I got close. Before he could cut me off, I said, "hey there, I'm Special Agent Colin Sharpe of the FBI. I live right next door here; can you tell me what's going on?" He said there had been a homicide in the house and me being me I asked, "you're positive it's a homicide"?

He chuckled and said, "Oh, I'm positive all right. Slip on some booties and come have a look but stay close to me." He was more cooperative than I would have expected from local law enforcement, but I WAS the neighbor after all. He would likely also assess me as a possible suspect at the same time.

He asked all the usual questions as we moved toward the front door. Had I heard anything? Did I recall any strange cars? Did I see anyone around the area who didn't belong? Was he having any issues I knew of? He stopped questioning me once I reminded him, I was with the bureau and that this neighborhood had always been safe. He apologized explaining it was a force of habit, sort of like me snooping around for information.

He gave me a running commentary as we walked through the house. No evidence of a struggle and it appeared two or three guys had beaten this fellow to a pulp. He showed me the bloody chair and lifted the sheet off the body. It was Bobby all right and he was an absolute mess. To be honest, I have seen a few mafia crime scenes, and this was quite similar, perhaps even more gruesome if that is even possible.

It certainly looked like someone had been trying to get information out of him. Valuable information by the looks of the beating and the time it would have taken. I wondered what could they want from Bobby? He seemed to be a good guy. I knew he worked with Jonathon and Luke and was a rather good surfer. I suppose that was about it. We were neighbors and friends, but it was obvious we were not that close. There was nothing to indicate this could be part of my case, but I had a nagging feeling that somehow it might be connected. I soon began to wonder if he was an abuser of women?

The locals were there for a quite a while. The coroner took the body out after they took all their photos, and the place was locked up. I caught the OIC out front before he left and handed him my card. I explained I didn't want to step on any toes but as the deceased was my friend and neighbor, I would really appreciate him sharing whatever information he could with me.

I really didn't expect to hear much and figured I would have to search on my own. That was easy enough to do for the FBI. We could pretty much look into any law enforcement case we wanted to on US soil, so I wasn't concerned. It made it easier though when he turned, shook my hand and introduced himself again saying," I'll definitely keep you posted, you federales can look anywhere you want so I might as well save you the hassle." We both laughed, and he went on to say that perhaps I might even be of some help on the background side of things.

It would have to be un-official, but we agreed to grab lunch the next day. I racked my brain thinking of things until the time came to meet. Business problems? Gambling debts? Pissed off client? Over my career, I have learned there are hundreds of reasons why people are killed. Some by accident, some on purpose. I also knew that as the facts presented themselves oftentimes the story would almost build itself.

Evidence would surface, connections would be made and eventually a motive would be understood. Once you had a motive identified it became much easier to find the perpetrator. I had no reason to think any different here, after all murder was murder. It could get complicated, but it wasn't rocket science.

I gathered my thoughts into my off-duty notebook. Off-duty notebooks were really frowned upon but a few of us still kept them. Keeping this out of the bureau's prying eyes would be a clever idea for now. If it turned out I needed the information for something official, I could easily transfer it into my own notebooks thereby keeping everything legitimate. I was eager to meet with Captain Sanchez, find out where they were and give him what little information that I had.

We met and spent a few minutes discussing generalities and then before I could start, he unloaded on me.

He said, as originally suspected, there was virtually no forensic evidence to be found. He said it was one of the "cleanest" crime scenes he had ever seen.

The body had been examined almost immediately and it was found the cause of death was internal bleeding caused by multiple blows to the head and body, mostly the body. It had taken him quite a while to succumb to the beating so whomever did this knew they had time.

The coroner had made a couple of key observations. The blows were very well placed and designed to inflict maximum pain without causing death too soon. He was beaten to death by someone who had done this before. Based on the damage, it was someone who had studied anatomy, or at least understood torture. He also said it appeared the deceased had been restrained in a chair for most of the beating. The last critical piece of information he added was that this was the work of one man and one man only.

Thanks to modern science, the coroner was able to determine the blows were all inflicted by one person. They were delivered with both the right and the left hands of the killer. He looked at me and said, "this guy is an absolute cold-blooded, trained killer. It looks like he was after information." I also noted he was ambidextrous as well. I was beginning to know a killer like that myself...

Wow, that was an interesting piece of information. I saw the scene up close and to think one person did that much damage was tough to comprehend. It was obviously a crime of passion or payback. I had seen some gruesome murder scenes in my day, but this one took it to a whole different level. I asked what they had found in the car, and he said it was gone. No surprise there. He had uploaded the information into his system already, but those vehicle bolos often took weeks to yield a result.

There were just too many cars in Los Angeles, and they could go un-noticed for an awfully long time. Many times, the vehicle was never found, having been completely parted out in a few days at a chop shop. Those guys were amazingly skilled at tearing down a vehicle and I always wondered if they could build them just as quickly?

I seem to recall a classmate or two in auto-shop in high school who looked like they were destined for just such a life.

I already doubted the car would yield any evidence, anyway, based on the fact there was nothing in the house. I told him about the girlfriend and the car she drove and told him I would keep an eye out.

I said my other neighbor worked with him and gave him Jonathon and Luke's phone numbers. I explained they had some sort of financial company, and they were all successful, according to what I knew.

I had decided not to mention anything about Meg at this point as they had been broken up for a while. I would, of course, have an opportunity to discuss it with her at the party. I planned to make my own assessment before telling anyone else. I was unsure whether I wanted to give her the benefit of the doubt or if I was worried about my own career. It would be a great time for a big win for me though.

Captain Sanchez and I chatted a little more about police work in general. I shared some details about the case I was working on, and he commiserated with me. We laughed about how the cake-eaters were always crawling up someone's butt and yet we were the ones who made them look good. They just sat back and watched while we did all the heavy lifting and then they took all the credit. It was a common topic of discussion when the rank and file gathered.

We left, vowing to keep in touch. I liked him. He was thorough, professional, and intelligent. I always respected top quality law enforcement people, even if they didn't always respect the bureau. Local law enforcement frequently saw the bureau as a thorn in their side or someone trying to steal the "good" cases from them.

Guys like Sanchez were always far more concerned about solving the crime. They saw all law enforcement as playing on the same team. They fully embraced the us against them mentality.

It was Thursday of that same week when I was out front cleaning up a bit and Bobby's girlfriend showed up. She was knocking on the door. She looked over and asked if I had seen Bobby and what was the police thing on the door about? She asked if he had been robbed and I suggested she come over for a glass of tea or something.

I knew I should have told her to call Captain Sanchez right away, but I also knew what I was doing. I brought her a glass of pop, and we chatted a bit. I said I hadn't seen Bobby for a few days. When I thought she was relaxed, I told her that Bobby had been killed and I watched for her reaction.

You cannot fake that kind of shock and response to news like that, so I immediately knew she had nothing to do with it. She broke down, sobbing loudly, while I consoled her. I asked if it would be okay if I asked her a few questions before I referred her to the locals.

It took her a while to calm down but eventually she did. I posed the usual questions like if she knew of any trouble that Bobby was in?

Had he said he had any issues at work? Did he gamble that she knew of? I covered all the bases and then decided to throw in my own curve. Who knows, my intuition has guided me more than once to the right answer.

I watched her face closely and asked if "Bobby had ever hit her or been rough with her?" She said no, but it was obvious to me she was holding something back. The creases around her eyes, her body language and the throbbing vein on her neck gave her away. She would be a lousy poker player I thought. She became a little shakier while explaining that he liked things his way and sometimes he could get a little mad. I gently prodded her, and she finally admitted that she did feel sometimes like he was controlling her and that he could get quite jealous at times.

I knew there was still more, it was just a matter of letting her share.

It took at least fifteen more minutes of discussion and consoling her before she finally said that he had indeed hit her. She said it only happened once, but I knew that was unlikely. She explained that he was deeply sorry and the next day he showed up at her office with two dozen roses and a big apology. He said it would never happen again, blah blah blah.

Exactly the things an abuser would naturally say and do. I lived next door to this bastard and didn't see it! Maybe I WAS losing my edge?

I should have seen the signs. It was Patti who said that I was always working, and I needed to find a way to just enjoy people. Had I heeded her advice and subsequently missed something?

While I was certainly going to pass this information along to Captain Sanchez, I had no intention of sharing the information that Meg had dated him. I would save that until after this weekend. I advised her to keep this to herself and then got her phone number, address and such and told her that Captain Sanchez or one of his detectives would contact her on Monday.

I walked her to her car and opened the door. After she drove away, I phoned Sanchez and left a message telling him I had an update and asking him to call me as soon as he could. I did not want to give the impression I was trying to get all up in his case, so I felt compelled to tell him I had spoken with the girlfriend.

Chapter Twenty 4 - The Casual "Interrogation"

Patti and I got ready to head over to the party. As usual we strolled down the beach letting the warm waves lap at our ankles as we walked. I knew she would be pissed, so I forewarned her I might ask a few casual questions related to the case. Everyone knew Bobby was dead by now and I just had to get a feel for things. After all, he was our neighbor.

Patti stopped dead in her tracks and told me to go on alone. If I was going to do my "cop-thing" at our friend's party she wanted no part of it. She wasn't particularly upset it didn't seem, but I knew she was not a fan when I got like this. She said she didn't want me pissing off our friends.

She told me she would be relaxing on the patio and that I should be home within three hours if I knew what was good for me. I explained that I did, and I would see her in precisely three hours. She smiled a sly smile and said, "don't make me start without you." She kissed me on the cheek and whacked my rear end as I walked away. She certainly got me, like nobody else ever had.

I went up the steps and saw Jonathon looking out at the ocean. He said how shocked he was Bobby was dead. He went on to say he had met with a detective who asked if Bobby was in any trouble at work? He asked him all kinds of questions about gambling and any enemies. Jon looked at me and said he had nothing to tell the guy. He was a good employee, number three in the company and they were all very successful. Together.

In fact, their clients were all doing very well, like Warren Buffett well, thanks to them. Bobby was a big part of the reason for that success. He just had a knack for picking winners and Jonathon couldn't remember a portfolio on the negative side that Bobby had handled. I just said they were all the typical questions, all standard. He added that he couldn't see this being work related. Nobody ever gets killed over making someone too much money.

I asked if they had noticed anything with the current girlfriend? Had there been any incidents during parties? Any jealous outbursts or anything like that. He said they really hadn't noticed anything but thought he might be considering breaking up with the new girlfriend. When I asked if he had any idea why, Jon said Bobby told him that she was being a little distant.

He also said something about wandering eyes. That would certainly be something that would bring out the worst in a guy like Bobby. The combination of indifference to the abuser and displaying any interest in another male would be like waving a red flag in front of a bull.

I wandered around saying hello to the people I knew while watching for Meg to arrive. Sure enough, as I sat in a chair by the water, she showed up carrying a beer. We exchanged pleasantries and I asked if she wanted to join me. She sat down, I turned to her and asked, "Did you hear about Bobby?" She said she had and went on to say how terrible that was. I said it must be strange to have an ex-boyfriend turn up dead. She said it most certainly was, looked me straight in the eye saying, "It was more than that, you may not have known, but I actually lived with him for a brief time."

She was obviously being open, so I thought one more question before I closed it off. "Did he ever hit you or was he verbally abusive at all?" It was a bit of a loaded question. It was highly unlikely the current girlfriend was the only woman he treated like that. These guys typically had a history of controlling or abusive behaviour.

Meg again looked me straight in the eye and said, "I don't want to speak ill of the dead, but he did hit me. Twice in fact. The second time was when I broke up with him and moved out, about three months ago." She added, "Generally, the split was amicable though and once I was gone, we had no other issues." She went on to share that she thought his new girlfriend seemed nice and asked if I didn't agree. She said we were frequently at the same parties right here, so somebody would have noticed if she was having a problem.

Interesting, she not only answered the question but gave me more than she was asked. That could happen for very innocent reasons, but it could also be subversive in nature and meant to confuse whoever was asking the questions. I would file that comment away for future reference.

I said I didn't want to bore her so asked how things were going in her life. We chatted for quite a while and had another beer each when Meg asked if I was a surfer too. I said I most definitely was, and she grabbed my hand and led me over to the boards. Out to the waves we went, and we spent about an hour or so chatting and riding. Each time she caught a wave in front of me I watched as she twisted and turned that perfect body, manipulating the board like a pro.

I was trying to keep those thoughts out of my mind but wasn't doing a particularly decent job of it. We had a couple more rides and then headed in to shore and showered next to each other in the outdoor shower. It was big enough for four people much less two and it's not like we were naked or anything. Everyone rinsed off here, that's why it was there.

Still, in my own tiny brain, I found myself wondering what it might be like to really shower with her. While we stood there washing off the salt water, I had visions of me playfully washing her all over.

I was trying to stare at the wall or out at the ocean, but I found myself trying to catch as many glances of Meg as I could. Pretending to turn towards the water to rinse myself off and admiring her while I was doing so. I had to leave and leave now.

I went inside to use the washroom and as I stepped out of the door, I found myself staring at Meg. She put her hand on my chest and I allowed her to push me back inside. The door closed, and she was kissing me before I really knew what was happening. I suppose I knew but just didn't want to think about it. I started to embrace her as we kissed but then stopped.

I pushed her back and she began to pull away at the same time. She was apologizing as much as I was and said she had too many drinks.

I said we both did, and I left quickly. Nobody had seen anything, but I still wondered if she was playing a game or not. She knew I was happily married but perhaps I was sending out some sort of signal?

Not long after that I said good-bye to everyone and quickly headed down the beach to our house. I walked through the house and found Patti on the upper patio as promised.

She was behind the pool and closer to the house, so nobody could see us.

I could see her glass was empty, so I grabbed a bottle of wine and as I got closer, she let her robe fall open revealing only skin. I wasn't sure if she knew something or not, but we finally went back into the house and over an hour later she knew that I loved her with all my heart and soul.

I knew from that moment on, I would never again touch Meg and I would force all thoughts of her from my mind the second they appeared. There was absolutely no way I was going to be THAT guy! There were enough of them in the law enforcement ranks as it was.

Over the years I had known all kinds of people in this "business", men and women, who had cheated. None that I knew ever ended up dead but not too many had a normal life afterward. Many times, the issues were a lack of common ground and the inability of the spouse to understand what we went through on a daily basis. This life was not meant for everyone and that includes spouses and significant others.

Patti and I did not have those challenges. We lived each other's successes and failures. Certainly, she helped me a lot more than I helped her. but we were a great team. There was many a case where she helped me to look pretty darn good.

Chapter Twenty 5 – Off to The Party

The party day arrived, and I set off for Kathy and Jon's. I was really hoping Special Agent Sharpe would be there. Colin had started to open up about his case a little the last time we met. I was really hopeful he might continue along that line. Now I had to find out just where he was at if I could. I needed to know if he had connected Bobby to the others yet or not.

I knew if he had or if the current girlfriend admitted to any abuse that I would be asked by someone eventually. I felt it more likely that it would be the local force, but I also knew that Colin would be interested. After all, the guy lived right next door and knew both of us! I decided this would be a fun little party after all. Whether Bobby was my last or not I would ensure that I knew absolutely everything about what was happening.

I got to the party, chatted with the girls a bit and then went to have a look around. I grabbed a Corona from the cooler and spotted Colin as I walked toward the sand. I said hello and sat down next to him. We were chatting for a bit when he mentioned Bobby and asked if I had heard anything about it. I said no, and he shared that it looked like he had been beaten up by a few guys.

The questions then seemed to be much closer to an interrogation than a discussion. Once a cop always a cop I figured. Sure enough, after a little while, he asked if Bobby had ever hit me. I figured the girlfriend had already come clean, so I told him very directly that he had. I even said it was more than once. I chuckled inside as he looked surprised that I had told the truth. What did he take me for, an idiot? There was no way some chump FBI agent was going to bring me down, friend or not. None of them had the skill set and it was plainly obvious.

We talked a little more and had another beer and I figured I would relax him out in the water. We each grabbed a board and paddled out to catch a few waves. This part of the beach was always good for nice sets of four and five footers that were easy to ride. You didn't need to think too hard or plan, just hop on and surf. We rode a few decent ones and then headed into shore and showered off.

It was a large communal shower out on the deck, so I thought nothing of both of us in there at the same time. I could tell he was doing his best to hide it, but he kept turning to look at me. I made sure I was really clean all over, so he could sneak more glances. I decided I would use his own interest to throw him off balance at my next opportunity.

We had a couple more beers each and I watched as he walked into the house. I figured he was most likely headed for the restroom.

I gave him a head-start and then slipped inside and down the hallway. I waited until I heard the door unlock and then stood right in front of it.

As the door opened, I stepped inside, put my hand on his chest and moved him back inside and then kissed him hard. I felt his arms around me, and his hands go straight to my butt. We kissed a little longer as he hugged me and then we pushed away from each other. We both began apologizing to one another the second we separated.We were blaming our behavior on the booze, the sun, the heat, you name it. We both said that would never happen again and we walked back outside quickly.

He left not long after, no doubt to run back to Patti to assuage his guilt. That was exactly what I wanted to happen. I didn't want him thinking about me and I didn't want him checking into me. It was almost impossible for anyone to dig up my information about my true past, but it was always good to keep extra safeguards in place. I didn't even want people looking into my life since I got out.

I was confident after that kiss and the way he responded to me he would keep his hands and mind off me. He seemed to be an honorable man and it was plain to see Patti was the love of his life. He likely thought I was just another beach girl who was all confused and I had caught him at a moment of temporary weakness.

That is exactly what I wanted him to think. I wanted him confident that I had neither the smarts nor the motive to pull this off. I knew that in situations like this, motive was everything. Too often, when the prosecution could prove motive, juries were never that far from convicting.

There are many innocent people in jail who were convicted based on completely circumstantial evidence simply because they had a REASON to kill someone else. It was one of the sad failings of our judicial system. It happens far more often than people realize.

Chapter Twenty 6 – My Work Is Simply Not Finished

I reviewed what I had done and what had driven me to do it. I knew it was wrong, but I also knew the justice system could not, or would not, protect these women. The system had already failed them so many times and there was no reason to believe it was going to improve. It appeared the burden now fell on me to take out as many as possible. I would tilt the scales of justice towards the victim instead of the criminal for a change.

I thought I wanted to stop but as I noticed more and more men over the coming weeks, I knew I couldn't stop my work yet. I was confident there were still no leads, and it was going to be nearly impossible to connect me, unless I made a serious mistake. The bottom line is that I just do not make serious mistakes. I had no plans to start making them now.

I went over my current strategy and tactics, reviewing the details on each of the five "situations" I had fixed to date. I determined that if I was going to find more of these guys that it was simply too dangerous to keep going to bars looking for them. There were too many variables that I could not control, and I liked being in complete control. It was always safer.

That is how I lasted as long as I had doing what I had been doing for our government. Controlling the situation and minimizing or changing variables was my stock-in-trade. It is what kept me alive.

I looked at a few options and determined the simplest and easiest way was just to ask who needed help. I created a site on the darkweb using more of my government developed skills. I could disguise the routing and location so that no matter how I was tracked, if I were ever tracked, nothing would lead back to me. I thought about routing through an FBI server for laughs but decided I didn't want them THAT angry! There was nothing to be gained by trying to make them look stupid. Agencies like them never took kindly to being publicly ridiculed, but then I suppose nobody did.

I stuck to my original plan and used an amazingly simple site setup with words that would attract battered and abused women. I targeted women who were likely at their wits end. Those who had perhaps already been to court, usually more than once. Those who felt they had very few options and were concerned for their lives. I decided that I would start with this and see what popped up. In the meanwhile, I would go about my life as usual. I kept training hard, running and honing my intelligence skills.

All the while I was doing this I was still going to the odd party at Kathy and Jonathon's and a couple at Luke's. Most interestingly, I even got invited to one at Colin and Patti's.

Everyone was going, and I was standing right there when they invited them. Patti smiled and said," you'll be there, won't you Meg?" That was an invitation that was simply too hard to resist.

I recall that party like it was yesterday. I started at Kathy's and then we just walked up the beach to Colin's house. Not sure if I forgot or even if I ever knew but I was shocked to see they lived right next door to Bobby's. Or at least Bobby's house, that is until he died that tragic and horrible death.

I smiled on the inside as we walked past the house, recalling the sight of him dying. Kathy said how odd it was without Bobby around and how she couldn't believe what had happened to him. I agreed how terrible it was and asked if they had spoken to his girlfriend at all. It sounded like they had not seen her for quite a while. She was likely as glad to be rid of him as I was.

The party started out uneventfully and everyone was just hanging out. It was exactly like the other parties as one would expect. Colin and Patti's house is much more modest than Kathy and Jonathon's though. Their yard wasn't even in the same zip code. It was so much more basic, but it did look out onto the Pacific. Now I knew why they were always over at Kathy's place. They did have a nice large deck off the upper floor of the house with a pool and everything, so they weren't exactly slumming, but there was little equality between the two homes.

I was wondering how an FBI agent and a detective profiler had the scratch to own an oceanfront home like this. As I walked past a small group, I overheard Colin telling them how lucky they were that his father left them this house. Ah, okay, he wasn't on the take then. Another tidbit of information that might come in handy down the road. The more facts and background you gathered on people, the simpler it became to read them and there was less likelihood of them gaining the upper hand. You had to know quite a few things about someone to build an accurate profile.

It had now been a couple of months since Bobby's death, and everything seemed to have returned to normal. We were all just sitting around, and the boys were talking about work. I thought that was a good opportunity to casually ask Colin how his case was going. I said there was only so much financial talk one could endure and asked what was happening with him these days.

My comment got no reaction other than him saying, "this could be one that doesn't get solved." I just left it at that as he didn't offer anything more and I certainly wasn't going to enquire any further.

I felt confident I was completely in the clear, but it was always good to verify. The talk quickly returned to capital markets, overseas investment in the USA and other topics I didn't really care to hear about.

Chapter Twenty 7 – The Next One

The party wrapped up and when I got home, I decided to check the drop box on my site. Sure enough, there was some contact information in there with a brief cry for help. A woman who claimed to live "somewhere in California" said she was within weeks of taking her own life. She had moved out. She had tried to hide, but this guy kept tracking her down. What was worse was that somehow, he would suck her back into his life and within weeks she was bruised again in one spot or another. She was scared and constantly in fear for her life and believed she had nowhere to turn.

She said she would do anything to find a way to hide from him and stay hidden. I contacted her back asking if there were any kids involved and a few other questions, so I could get a baseline of where she was at. I needed to find out if she would be open to the "ultimate solution" to her problem. There were numerous ways I could get the information and I decided the best way would be to send her to a payphone. I would call her using my voice changer and interview her that way.

Rather than scramble the voice or garble it up the voice changer made my voice sound exactly like a white male, around age 30. The built-in firmware was complex so that there was no way to determine the words were not being spoken as is.

It was also impossible to unscramble the voice and bring it back to mine. It was the same box I used to fool that woman in the car when I eliminated her problem and one I had used many times while in the forces. I sent her an address and a time to be there. I knew the spot and knew that I could very easily set up across the street in my car and be completely invisible. I would have a clear view of her though and could get a photo or two as well.

I got to the parkade about an hour early to ensure there was nothing odd going on prior to the call. There were no people sitting in vehicles for too much time, no walkers circling the block, nothing out of the ordinary. I watched as a lady pulled up in a car just before two and I recorded the license plate for later. She got out and stood by the phone at exactly 2:00 PM so I knew that was my girl.

She picked up on the first ring and said she only had about fifteen minutes, he was likely going to check on her. She was almost in tears, and I had to take some time to calm her down. She asked what I was going to do about him. I told her I could gather a few friends and "convince" him to leave her alone. She told me that wouldn't be enough, her three brothers had already tried that. She told me restraining orders didn't help either and she would do anything to be free of him.

I calmly asked her if she would be happy if he simply disappeared?
    She would never hear from him or see him again and I could guarantee for her that would be the case. She just said, "how much?" I was a little concerned when she responded that way. Most people, even those in her position, would usually be somewhat aghast when presented with such an option. Fortunately, her story would be easy to check out.

I told her that my services were free of charge, I just wanted to help women get out of trouble. I said it was in honor of my mother, and this was my way of giving back. I got a few more details and told her to please act as if nothing was out of the ordinary. I was convinced she could do that and then told her this was the last time we would speak. She was crying as she said good-bye. I watched her get into her car and drive away and I scanned the area for another fifteen minutes before I left.

I went back to my house and fired up my equipment to begin checking into this woman. I tracked the plate through the DMV database and from that got her driver's license number. The picture matched her as did all the details, so I recorded the address and got ready for surveillance.

Interestingly, the address was in a nice area called Montecito. It is basically a suburb of Santa Monica. It sure wasn't like the dive areas I had found the other targets in. Montecito was a very upscale locale, lots of rich folks and multi-million-dollar mansions. Just goes to show that abuse of women happens everywhere and that perhaps no woman is truly safe.

This might be a little tougher than I expected. These folks typically had expensive and complex security systems. They also seemed to like keeping guard dogs around and other security measures, depending on how wealthy they were.

I started gathering the intel I would need via the internet. I knew my good old Russian routing trick would come in handy later in life.

I was able to access virtually any database, site, email, or other online format that I wanted without anyone ever knowing or even being able to find out it was happening.

I had to find a way to secretly observe what was really happening and confirm this wasn't some money scam or insurance deal. Thanks to my prior life I knew how to hack into smart TV's, computer cameras and almost anything else that was "connected". After hacking their Wi-Fi network, in a little over an hour, I had access to all those devices inside their house. I was now able to see exactly what was happening whenever I wanted to.

The internet is a wonderful thing but very few people realize how dangerous it can be. If people knew that when someone like me had the skills and equipment, we could use their own cellphone camera to watch them they might not have their phone with them 24 hours a day.

The only thing was I couldn't risk recording anything so whatever I did was basically live streamed. I would watch as it was happening and then it was gone. I always had my good old pencil and paper close at hand though!

It took a few days of peeking in every now and then and seeing things I really did not want to see. It was late on a Friday, and I wasn't sleeping so I decided to check in via their security webcams. About an hour in, when I was ready to give up, I watched as they both came in the front door. They were well dressed and had obviously been at some high-end event. Almost as soon as the door was closed the façade disappeared. He yelled at her about dancing with "that ass" and then, out of nowhere, slapped her hard on the back of the head. My first thought was this jerk was smart enough to hit where there were no bruises and no damage to her face. What a pig!

She staggered away telling him not to touch her again. Clearly, he had other ideas as he moved toward her and smacked her again, this time on the side of the head. You could see she was staggering and hurt, likely a mild concussion. I watched a few more minutes on the other cameras but I had already seen enough. I decided right then how I would take this clown out. I shut off the feed and began planning. It wouldn't be as gruesome as Bobby, but it would not be quick either.

I needed do some further sleuthing before I could move ahead with any plan though. I had left a few sniffers on her own systems, so I could ensure with 100% certainty I wasn't being trapped. The next day one of the sniffers kicked back to me a possible concern in a message on her cellphone. I was looking for any words, phrases or IP addresses that were in any way connected to law enforcement people or sites. The software watched for those words in all electronic communications to or from that source.

It is the same way the Department of Homeland Security knows when to watch certain individuals they think might be terrorists. The power that outfit has to watch, listen in on and read communications between ALL Americans would shock you. They trample all over the fourth amendment as if it did not even exist.

Of course, the framers of the constitution had no idea how the world would change in the coming centuries. After all, the fourth amendment was ratified, as part of the Bill of Rights, in December of 1791. At that time there was no CIA, no FBI and in fact law enforcement consisted only of a loose collection of regular people. It resembled today's citizens on patrol groups much more than it did any organized law enforcement. I shouldn't fault DHS though; I suppose I had nothing to stand on when talking about ends justifying means. I had vacated the high moral ground long ago.

Sure enough, there was an encrypted message that had come in to her cellphone from an IP address in a law firm.

It could be nothing, but I certainly was not about to take a chance. I decrypted the message and was flabbergasted when I saw an email that contained a signature with her name followed by ATTORNEY-AT-LAW!

It went on to say she specialized in criminal cases. She was a freaking DEFENSE LAWYER. What on earth was going on here? Was this some sort of trap? The video I saw at her house could not have been staged, and there was absolutely no way she could have known I was eavesdropping. Also, those slaps did damage, they weren't for show.

She clearly had constructed an elaborate ruse built to hide the fact she was a lawyer. It was just as obviously done for the sole purpose of contacting me. Why else would someone create an alternate identity?

I decided right then and there that I would simply drop it and not follow up at all. I went about deleting all trails that might potentially lead to me, even though I was certain nothing could. I felt I had dodged a bullet and was not about to stick my head out the window again.

Chapter Twenty 8 – The Waiting Game

That was an interesting narrow escape. I decided to wait a month or two before doing anything else. In the meanwhile, I would go back to what I had been doing all along. I would stick to my schedule. Run, weight train and keep myself sharp. Just life as usual in sunny SoCal.

Of course, that also involved hanging out with Kathy and Angela and their respective husbands from time to time. It was always good to meet Colin and Patti at their parties too. I could watch and listen for any more clues on his big case and would hopefully be warned in advance if there was anything I should be concerned about. I had no reasons to be worried but being vigilant had kept me alive so far, why would I stop now?

The last time I bumped into them, Special Agent Sharpe seemed particularly down in the dumps. The party was going well, and everyone was having a fun time, but Colin didn't seem as into it as the rest of us. I strolled over to where he was sitting and said, "hey, why the long face?"

Before he could answer Patti looked up at me and said, "oh, he's just a little pissy because the bad guy seems to have gotten away." He was obviously not impressed by that comment as he didn't even crack a smile.

I was again close to asking if he was sure it was a guy but didn't think poking the bear was such a great plan.

I think I was actually a little offended that the assumption was that it had to be a male. I smiled and asked them both what they were drinking and got them each one. I set the drinks down in front of them and said, "life's way too short to worry about the odd failure. Focus on the wins." Patti smiled up at me, looked over at Colin and rephrased what I had just said. As one would assume, he wasn't at all soothed by our comments.

I walked away happy about the whole situation. I was confident I was completely in the clear and untraceable, but I DID like getting that second opinion every now and then. In my line of work being compulsive had never been a hindrance to success. The party was still a lot of fun, but I was glad to get home to my own bed this night.

Life kept moving on and after what I felt was the right amount of time, I decided I would again look at my site on the darkweb. There were a couple of messages there this time but the one from "battered1" stood out. She must have figured out I knew she was a lawyer, why mail me back? I opened the message and read it a few times start to finish.

"Dear Helper: I realize that by now you have uncovered who I really am. That does not concern me in the least. What concerns me is that I thought we had an agreement. I appreciate that you are wondering what I am doing and whether this is a trap? I can assure you it is not a trap. I will leave it up to you to have me contact you any way you want, any where you like at any time of your choosing.

I would like to talk to you more about what you do. I think there are things we can do together to make the world a safer place for women." I read and reread the message a few times before closing it. That last line is what really caught my interest. It drew me back in. I sensed, based on all my experience, that this woman had a story to tell. I knew at that moment we would meet in person, sooner rather than later. I also knew that there would be no plan, no calls, no notes, nothing. I would catch her at a time when she was alone, could not be watched or monitored and I could ensure we were able to have the conversation I wanted.

I planned our meeting for at least a month later. I tracked every movement she made, listened to every phone call she had and read each text and email sent from either of her phones. I saw absolutely nothing other than work and client communications and the normal personal stuff one would expect.

I knew where she went to the gym and decided it was likely one of those spin classes where somebody yells at you to ride harder. Not my thing, but I suppose some people needed that. It was a social thing too, so I knew there would be a group that trained together frequently. People always dropped their guard when they were in a group. Civilians anyway. The groups I had been part of were always on ultra-high alert even when we were together, we never dropped our guard.

I made my plan. I knew when she trained there, and I knew the route she would use to go home, nine times out of ten anyway. I then patiently waited for the right day to come. I watched her arrive and park her car. I waited about fifteen minutes to give her time to get into her "workout".

There were no surveillance cameras and very few people seen going in and out of that area of the garage. They were probably all doing the same thing and felt comfortable parking together. What they saw as safety in numbers I knew was an opportunity to work without interruption.

I grabbed my tools and quickly drilled a 4 mm hole in her oil line. I had calculated that she could travel between 30 and 40 miles before the engine would shut down. When it did, I would be there to pick her up. I left and got about fifteen miles away on her usual route home and waited for her car to pass by. I could also easily see if she were being followed by anyone, so I could bide my time. I didn't want to be seen following her right from the gym as with all the traffic cameras around it could pose a problem.

I parked my car along the route and watched my rear-view mirror. I checked out each car as it passed. I didn't have to wait too long until I saw her car approaching. I let her drive past as I confirmed she was the driver, and she was alone. I knew the route, so I just waited. I saw there were no vehicles behind her.

I pulled out slowly and headed on the same route.

Chapter Twenty 9 – A Shock

Maybe ten minutes later, I saw her car pulled over on the side of the road. She was standing on the sidewalk next to it. She was not on the phone yet, so I pulled up next to her, stopped and yelled through the passenger window. I knew if she heard a woman's voice, she would approach the car. As she got to the window, I had a gun held low across my chest, pointed at the window. She leaned in as I said, I'm your helper, don't say a word. I then directed her to get in the car or be shot.

I thought it was very odd that she smiled when I said that. She looked over and said, "I was wondering when you would show." I told her to open her vest, pull up her shirt and lean forward. I needed to ensure there were no listening devices anywhere. I also had a scanner sitting on the dash and it confirmed there were no devices listening or sending signals that could be tracked.

I glanced at her while I started to drive and said, "You're a lawyer, why the hell do you want your husband to disappear? Can't you get rid of him in a court of law?" She looked at me and said, "because he beats me but that's not the only reason. If you're as good as you seem to be I think we could possibly work together." I now knew that I had her dead to rights if I wanted, so we were already in this together.

I determined I could safely speak frankly with her and see where this might take us. When I saw her up close like this I decided very soon that she could be trusted. At this point the gun was superfluous so I just put it away and held out my right hand to shake hers.

I told her we should talk more in depth about this and suggested a stop on a quiet section of beach. She agreed, and we drove off. When we parked and were walking to the beach, she told me I needed to show her I wasn't bugged either. I turned towards her and lifted my shirt. She looked me up and down, said "nice" and that was it. A bit odd I thought but I appreciated her being concerned too.

We sat on the beach for at least a couple of hours talking about everything. She explained that she was sick and tired of getting charges thrown out against guys she knew were guilty. Hell, some were even admitting their guilt to her and then she had to defend them, vigorously.

She wished she were not so good at defending criminals, but the career path had found her, not the other way around. When she was called to the bar, she soon discovered that she was built for litigation, and especially talented as a defense lawyer. The firm she worked at basically would not let her go any other direction once her skills became obvious.

They knew that she would make the firm a ton of money defending the worst of the worst. She went on to tell me how terrible it made her feel. She was exceptionally good at her job, but her job sometimes ended up putting guilty people back on the streets to beat, rape or kill again.

She told me what put her over the edge finally was that a jerk she got released went back after his accuser. Three days after he was back on the street, she was found strangled. A very nasty killing, and it was obvious it took her a long time to die. She was sick to her stomach when she heard what happened. She began to seriously question her choice of career.

Coincidentally, it was only shortly after that when her newish husband started to be abusive and controlling. When he began to be physically abusive, she already knew the courts were not the answer. He would likely end up with a lawyer as skilled as she was and would probably get off scot-free.

She felt trapped, and even though she made a lot of money and could easily run, she knew she would never be safe from him. That was when she began her search and eventually found me. When I went dark after our initial contact, she explained that she decided simply to wait as long as she could. If I didn't call, she was going to find a way to do it herself.

She had never killed anyone but had started going to the library to anonymously look up various poisons. There were a surprisingly large number of poisons one could use to kill another human being that would be difficult to track. Of course, being the spouse, she knew she would be the one the police would look at first. It would be too difficult and dangerous.

She was also well aware that poison was the weapon of choice when women killed, so all eyes would be on her if he died that way. It was too much to risk, but she was close to trying anyway. That's how desperate she was. Here were two women sitting alone on a dark beach wondering how truthful the other was being. Almost as if on cue, two bozos came up to us to chat us up. They started telling us how two beautiful women shouldn't be alone on the beach at night.

They said it was a dangerous part of the beach too. The usual bunch of BS. I was going to tell them to just leave us alone when they made a move to attack us.

The bigger one moved to grab me and the smaller one went for Norie. I told Norie not to move as I disabled my guy. I think his buddy was even more stunned as he watched me take the outstretched arm of his rather large friend and flex it around the guy's own head. I was choking him out with his own arm. I waited until he went limp and then stood up. The other guy just kept hold of Norie.

I told him there was no need to harm Norie. I said if he let her go, I wouldn't hurt him. Guys are SO predictable, and he did exactly as I expected. The challenge to his vaunted manhood was too much for him to ignore. I could see the thoughts right through his dense, beady little eyes. No girl is going to show me up he was thinking. I'll teach her a lesson he said to himself. He had no idea he was the one about to learn a painful lesson.

He threw Norie aside and came towards me. He reached out to grab me with a dirty, tattooed arm and I quickly turned the tables. A quick twist directly opposite of how the elbow usually bends and he was soon to be done. In seconds he was screaming like a baby as the bone in his elbow burst through the skin. Norie wanted to go but I made her just stay there with me as this guy was screaming and yelling that his arm was broken, which it was of course. However, it was much more than a simple broken arm that would heal easily.

The damage I had done to his elbow meant that particular arm would never work the same again. He had an incredulous look on his face, shocked at what I had done to him. He would have a painful reminder for the rest of his life. I wanted to wait there so I could watch one dolt scream in pain as the other woke up.

I liked to see that look of resignation when they looked up and saw a woman and knew, at least the quasi-smart ones knew, that if I wanted, they were dead. I smiled at Norie and said, "just a few more minutes, I like this part."

Finally, Tweedle-dee awoke and looked over at Tweedle-dummer who was now just whining as I let him try to slow the bleeding from his destroyed elbow. I could see the big guy giving a brief thought to coming after me again. I calmly pointed to his buddy saying," one move towards either of us and I will make both your arms look like your friend's there." You won't even be able to wipe your own butt. He looked at me closely and decided I was quite capable of hurting him much more than I already had. They helped each other to their feet and took off down the beach without another look back.

Norie looked at me and said, "you ARE the real deal, aren't you?" I just smiled and asked to hear more about her idea as we walked casually back to the car.

She wanted to know about me and my background, and I told her I don't share that information with anyone. I also said it would be safer for her if she did not know anything more about me. She seemed to understand why and my display of talent against two men closed the subject.

She reiterated that she was at her wits end, without a doubt. She felt that if he were not gone within a couple of months that she would surely turn up dead somewhere.

Chapter 30 – My Husband Next

After that night, Norie and I spent a lot of time together. I got the impression she was almost gay, but we never talked about anything like that. I had no intention of telling her I was "sort of Bi" so that was where that stayed. I determined we would focus on situations and outcomes and leave anything else alone...at least for now anyway. On any given day I was never sure where I sat on that subject, and it did frequently change. That was the one area of my life where I was confused, lacking a solid plan. My experience with Bobby did nothing to help me decide one way or the other.

We got down to the business of planning her husband's disappearance. She was really wanting to be there and watch which, at first, I did not see happening. She also wanted me to stretch it out and make the pain last, the way the pain he had inflicted on her had lasted. While my first reply was, "I don't really do torture," in my head I could already hear his bones cracking. Each shot followed by a grunt then the look of intense pain spreading slowly across his countenance. I had crossed over the torture threshold long ago and might as well accept that I did like it, at least when it was required to achieve closure. I finally relented, and we mapped out a complete plan. Now we simply needed to wait for the right day.

I determined the safest way to keep Norie in the clear would be a boating accident in the ocean.

I knew an area that typically had schools of sharks looking for something to eat. Groups of sharks can also be referred to as a frenzy of sharks, which is more what I had in mind. Their own little feeding frenzy, snacking on a dirt bag. Once there was blood in the water, I don't think sharks cared on what they were feasting.

Sharks are an interesting fish. This part of California is home to a large, natural white shark nursery and the population has been increasing in recent years. In 1994 the state began protecting sharks, so their numbers began to grow. Their favorite food source is sea lions and the resurgence of those populations combined with that protection meant there were now more white sharks than ever.

While Great Whites stick to eating sea lions, seals, and other smaller fish they are also opportunistic feeders. They will eat just about anything that may taste good. Humans may hunt sharks for various uses, but sharks typically do not hunt humans. However, if presented with the right set of circumstances all bets are off.

Almost all shark attacks on humans in California have been by Great Whites. There have been no fatal attacks since 2012 when surfer Francisco Solorio Jr was attacked and killed at Surf Beach in Lompoc. He was killed by a great white estimated to be 15 to 16 feet in length. One can only imagine how horrific such a death would be.

Razor-sharp teeth shredding your skin like paper, massive powerful jaws clamping down on limbs and tearing you apart.

Mercifully, in the case of fatalities, they were usually over quickly. I found that speed of death was no longer a concern of mine, at least not from the perspective of being quick. Prior to Francisco there had been one death by shark in 2010 and before that one in 2008. In total there have been more than one hundred shark attacks on humans in California since the state began tracking such incidents. The vast majority of those were non-fatal thanks to victims being able to fight back. They were not dead with one bite.

IF, and only if, a shark attacks should you fight back. Try to stay out of its way and know that it is impossible for even Michael Phelps to outswim a shark. If the shark is coming at you to attack, there are three vulnerable areas to aim at. Hard blows to the snout, eyes or gills will signal that you are not an easy meal. Kicks, punches and elbows will all work and may save your life. The shark will oftentimes decide to seek out an easier target.

For our purposes, this victim will be unable to fight back. When we toss him overboard, he will be a sitting duck, in a sea lion sort of way. One of the amazing facts about sharks is that they can sense blood in the water from over three (3) miles away!

We won't have to wait around too long to see the end either. Mature Great Whites can swim up to fifteen miles per hour. They are easily attracted by chumming the waters. Of course, in this case the victim will be the chum.

We needed two boats for the plan to work. I knew where I could acquire a second boat. I had been monitoring the marina close to me and I had a good idea of schedules. There seemed to be a lot of people in Southern California who owned boats but used them sparingly. I could easily grab one without anyone knowing for at least a week or two. I had already selected a basic, run of the mill boat that fit the bill.

Norie would work on getting her husband out for a day on the water so they could "get back on track." Once they were where I wanted them, and I confirmed there were no other craft for miles, I would pose as a broken-down boat. They would come over to help, I would quickly disable her husband and then we could get to work.

We didn't have to wait long for the perfect day. Nice enough to get out on the ocean but not so nice that every idiot and his dog was out there. We put our plan into motion. Norie said her husband seemed quite excited about a day on the water so they could get close again. They were certainly going to get close, but not at all in the way he was thinking.

I had preprogrammed a location into the GPS, disguised as a fishing spot, so Norie would know where to turn on the charm. I had a bag of "tools" with me on my boat and I motored out to the predetermined spot. I was happy to see there were no boats anywhere near, so I expected we would be safe. I dropped anchor and waited until I saw their boat approaching. I put out a couple of downriggers and two larger rods so anyone seeing us would think we were just fishing. I had even purchased a fishing license just in case we got stopped. You know my motto! It was definitely the only thing I had in common with the Boy Scouts.

I knew I could not use a flare as the risk of attracting unwanted attention was far too high. I didn't want two or three boats coming to rescue me and certainly did not want to attract the Coast Guard.

I thought I spotted Norie and her husband. As they became more visible, and I confirmed it was them, I raised my SOS flag. A black square and a black circle on an orange background. Every boater recognized this as a distress signal, and I had told Norie what to look for to be positive.

Sure enough they spotted the flag and turned towards me. Once they were close enough, I waved to them and then lowered my flag. I did not want any extra attention!

It was a little chilly and overcast but I was wearing my little black bikini as Norie knew that would distract him and keep him off guard. As I held out my hand to him, I could tell he was indeed very distracted.

His dark eyes barely left my chest. I pulled him on board and said I thought I had an oil leak, could he take a look? Being all gallant about it he said sure, he knew a lot about engines. Like most guys he probably didn't have a clue, but they were always willing to try and fool a woman it seemed.

He looked like your total California sailor-dude, or at least pseudo-sailor. His perfectly coiffed, curly hair blowing slightly in the breeze above a pastel-colored Boss golf shirt. A matching pair of shorts and docksiders on his feet completed the "look". He seemed like a caricature one might see in a TV ad for Southern California or Newport Rhode Island.

If one squinted, you could have been looking at a Kennedy, not Jack though. He was very distinctive.He had no idea what hit him. His foot landed on the lower deck as I connected solidly with a roundhouse to the head. When he came to, he was zip-tied to the center console, his arms secured tightly around the short mast behind him. His feet were firmly affixed to the same mast. The advantage of this rather than a chair was he would be completely unable to move and was braced solidly from the waist down. More importantly, for our purposes, his upper body and head remained relatively free.

He came to as I sat patiently across from him. Norie was directly behind him where she could not be seen, sitting quietly. He began to struggle but in short order realized he was totally immobilized.

He was yelling and screaming at me to let him go, asking what I was doing and who the hell I thought I was. He said he had a lot of money and so did his wife. She would pay a large ransom to save him. He went on to say she was a successful lawyer and would pay whatever I wanted.

I smiled at him and said I was a friend of his wife's and I thought that unlikely to happen. His eyes revealed he was beginning to comprehend what was going on. I moved beside him and struck him hard enough on the back of the head that I knew he would see stars, but not hard enough to seriously hurt him.

I smacked him again a couple more times. Norie then stepped out from behind him and the look on his face was priceless. He started calling her a bitch and said he would get her. I grabbed his head, looked him in the eye and explained that he WAS going to die and that it could take a few hours or a few days. He was certainly dying today, the only thing in question was how much it would hurt and how many times we would have to revive him.

I had warned Norie to stay away from his head when I outfitted her with some leather gloves and a short bat. The bat had a fairly good diameter and a soft covering but was easily heavy enough to break bones. The thing is the way it was padded allowed you to inflict maximum damage without killing or even breaking skin. It could be used anywhere on the body but was certainly best on extremities and body blows.

That was where this tool really shone as a weapon of human destruction. You could stretch pain and broken bones on for days if one wished.

He kept yelling as she brought the first hard blow down onto his forearm. This little woman had power and it was clear the arm was broken. He screamed out in pain and changed from threatening to apologizing and already begging for his life. It was always so disgusting when abusive men did this, so weak.

I had been in similar positions a few times and not once did I beg for anything. Not once did I scream out or cry. I would look impassively at my captors while I planned, making them believe I was resigned to die. I simply disconnected to enable me to plan my escape, my resolve buoyed and driven by the pain. I used that pain to motivate me to free myself with the sole purpose being to exact my revenge. In my case, revenge was never a dish served cold and I enjoyed it that way. Immediate gratification was the way to go for me.

Norie looked at him closely asking if he liked being hit? Did he enjoy the pain? He started saying he loved her, he was so sorry, he would never touch her again. She laughed and said he was correct; he WOULD never hit her again. But not out of choice. She struck a hard blow against the side of his ribs. She took a little off that one I thought, and she likely only bruised the ribs, which would make it painful to take deep breaths.

I was glad she didn't risk breaking a rib which could puncture a lung and cut short our "work".

I got up in his face again and told him what a pig he was and that guys like him were such jerks. I smiled at him and said his new name would be shark-bait, because that is what he would soon become. Before he could say anything, I drove my boot down on the top of his bare toes, breaking at least three. His screams were piercing, and I took a quick look at the radar to make sure there was still nobody within range. If so, we would have to gag him but that wasn't the case. Norie got to listen to him cry and beg for his life for a little while longer.

As she distracted him, talking about the way he hit her to disguise his dirty work, I hit him hard from the other side. I knocked out two teeth and he was bleeding pretty good. I smiled and said I didn't care how he looked because when we were done, and before he died, he would fulfill his destiny and become shark-bait. I described for him in detail how sharks fed, the razor-like teeth ripping and tearing flesh. Internal organs and muscles exposed to act as appetizers to the main course for the massive killer fish.

Norie gave him a few more shots and he was now bleeding internally as well. She hit him a few more times in the head, so I know he was feeling serious pain.

We lost the fun of it after about another half hour and as he slumped down, I untied him. Norie needed him to go in the water conscious. We carried him out to the deck. It was starting to get dark, so we chummed the waters around the boat. I was pleased to see sharks circling almost immediately. That was something you could always count on; sharks were always willing to eat.

Norie looked into his eyes and said what a scumbag he was and told him she hoped the sharks would use him as an appetizer for a few hours. I knew that wasn't going to happen. Once he was in that water, they would likely tear him apart in less than a minute. We flipped him over the edge and listened contently as the sharks devoured him completely in no time at all. Even in the almost darkness you could see the water turn blood red topped off by pinkish foam generated by the thrashing of the sharks as Norie's problem disappeared forever.

Once it was obvious the sharks work was complete, we started the boats up and moved a little way away. We went back to her boat and flipped the swim platform down. I jumped back into the "messy" boat and left Norie. She was to send up a flare and issue an SOS in fifteen minutes, no sooner and no later. I moved off at a fairly good speed closer to shore.

I had a safe spot to park the boat when I could go back in a couple of days and then take it out, bleach it and sink it. Once it was called in stolen that would be that.

Norie was to say that they were doing some romantic swimming to get reconnected. She got back in the boat to get wine while her husband swam a bit more. She heard her husband scream when she was in the cabin. She thought he was joking and told him what a jerk he was for faking being in distress. She went up to the edge of the boat and watched in horror as he was pulled under by a real shark. She didn't see him again after that moment, but the water turned red quickly.

The Coast Guard arrived within a half hour of the distress call and secured her boat to theirs. Being a lawyer, and therefore very skilled at stretching the truth, they seemed to have no concerns about Norie. They clearly believed her story.

I monitored several computers at the Malibu precinct, coast guard and an FBI channel and saw nothing to indicate anything other than a terrible accident. The papers reported it as such the next day. Further research by the police would reveal she had her own wealth, and they lived a happy, at least in public, life in Montecito. They would find no motive and she would be off the hook.

Nevertheless, we had agreed on no contact for two months. I went out two days later and retrieved the boat I had stolen. I bleached and washed that thing so well I likely could have sold it. I got to a secluded area in that part of the Pacific and made the boat ready for sinking. It would need to be found as having been intentionally sunk after a theft. Authorities would assume it was stolen, used for a few drug drops, and then disposed of to get rid of any evidence.

The simplest "stories" were always the best ones to tell. They made the most sense when there was no evidence to support any other theories.

Law enforcement agencies typically used this Occam's Razor theory when looking at most cases. This is the concept that when you have competing hypothetical answers to a problem that the one having the fewest assumptions is the most likely. It's basically a "stick to the facts" kind of thing and I knew that law enforcement was pre-disposed to think like that, unless anomalous evidence showed up.

The two locations were far enough away that even if the boat were discovered quickly, which was unlikely, the two incidents would never be connected. I got the dingy ready, motor prepped and ensured the gas supply was good. I tied it off to the engine of the boat, so my getaway would be smooth. I started the motor and left it at idle while I got back into the big boat.

As I needed it to look like an intentional sinking the simplest approach was to disconnect the bilge pump, unscrew the drain plug from the back and shoot a few holes into the bottom of the hold for good measure. A nine mm round leaves a large hole when it rips through fibreglass. I took care of the bilge pump and then shot a few holes in the bottom of the boat.

The water began coming in a little more quickly than I expected. That was good, less chance of anyone seeing, although it was nighttime so that made it easier too. I stepped off the sinking boat into the dinghy and reached over and pulled out the drain plug. I undid the rope and idled away as I watched the boat take on water and sink lower and lower.

All the hatches were left open including the portholes in the cabin, so the boat got heavy very quickly. It tipped and then sunk into the depths as I motored toward the beach about two miles up current. Nobody would give this abandoned small boat a second glance and it would either be scooped up by a larger craft or it would simply disappear at sea. Either way I was good. I beached it, hopped out and then decided to leave it there rather than set it afloat. I thought that would increase the likelihood of someone stealing it or at least borrowing it for the night.

I walked along the beach and up to a parking area. I got into my car without being noticed by anyone and drove calmly back home. No big deal. I pulled into my garage and gave this next phase of my life some consideration as I chilled with a nice bottle of wine.

All in all, I thought it had gone quite well but I had some concerns about my enjoyment while we were slowly killing Norie's husband.

I usually didn't let emotions creep into my work. I suppose that was easier when the people were simply targets, military or otherwise, who were threats to national security or something similar. Getting my own revenge was one thing but that had now expanded to getting revenge for others.

I finished the wine and dozed off where I was. I didn't even make it to my bed, but I was comfortable so why move? I had a great sleep, as I usually did after a successful mission.

It was time for a couple more months of regular socializing, being seen on runs and workouts and that type of thing. I liked returning to my somewhat normal life for a few months. It was a long wait until Norie and I could meet again. I was anxious to see how she was doing and what the plan would be. I would find out soon enough.

It was fun to hang with the girls though, attend a few gatherings and scout around for what might be available. I found that I seemed to be growing tired of the men I was being introduced to. I also noticed my thoughts were turning to Norie, and not always about "work".

She was an extremely attractive, successful woman. She was at least part Asian, and I found her features pleasing and still remembered when I was checking her for a wire. She was very pretty which went along nicely with her intelligence and no BS attitude. I also remembered her comment about me, but I pushed those thoughts out of my mind as best I could. I did not want to be weighed down by any relationships as, in too many cases, that could lead to failure and capture.

Romantic involvement with a co-worker or partner never seemed to work out well for anyone. I had seen too many people fail in their professional lives because of someone in their personal sphere.

If we were to be successful, we would need to stay focussed. Muddying up the waters with a relationship could be bad for "business".

Chapter 30 One – Nuts and Bolts

After what felt like an interminable wait, it was time to get to work again and find out what the deal was going to be. How would we identify the best targets? How would we implement our plans and what would we do to keep everything under wraps? I certainly was not about to get myself caught because I took on a partner, so extra caution would be necessary. Those killers who had partners always seemed to get caught more often than someone acting alone.

Two months had passed, and it was time for Norie and I to get together. I spent the week prior watching for any chatter and scanning both her cell phones. I still had sniffers on the internet connections at both our houses and there was absolutely no suspicious activity. I felt completely safe meeting at this point.

I decided she should come to my house, so on a Tuesday night she came over. I opened the door, she stepped inside, and we hugged. I felt I had a met a true kindred spirit and we both agreed we had missed the other person. That out of the way, I wanted to know much more detail about what she thought we should do.

Norie reiterated how my original method of targeting scumbags was dangerous and unpredictable. It was, and I readily agreed with her assessment. Norie told me she had access to various databases, not only her own cases. She told me there were a few of her own where she had gotten guilty men discharged and those were the ones she wanted off the street most. There was no need for abuse or torture, they just needed to go away.

I pointed out how we could lay out a trail leading to her own cases that would make it look like Russians or someone else hacked into her file server. It was very unlikely the connection would be made but preparation was always the key to success. At some time, it would surface that the men who were dying were clients of hers. For that reason, we planned the bread crumb trail.

We also looked at men for whom she had secured verdicts of innocent who had plenty of enemies. This might include other women who were abused or men with whom they had shady businesses and contacts. This was easy enough to track as we had all the files and the information nearby. It was unlikely they would look seriously at a lawyer being the perpetrator, but you know my motto.

I was excited about this new method and if I am being honest, I was excited to have a partner as driven to help the world as I was.

I knew we would be better together. I felt a little badly that I was keeping my background from Norie, but it was better this way. Better for both of us.

I killed my darkweb site and erased all traces that could even remotely connect me. It was unlikely I would need that again. Norie and I got together about a week later and she brought a file with her of a real winner. He was another rich guy who seemed unable to keep his hands off women. She had defended him, and he had gotten off on a technicality. Double jeopardy was attached so even though information that would have convicted him showed up later he remained free as a bird. Free to seemingly do whatever he wanted to whomever he wished.

Yup, Robert Stanley was a real piece of work, just the kind I enjoyed hunting and terminating. These guys were not completely dissimilar from the scumbags I had eliminated during my special forces career. They still did bad things, simply different bad things. They deserved to die, just as they had figuratively or literally killed their own partners.

Norie had lost a great deal of sleep over this one. He had confessed to her about one other situation as well as the girlfriend-beating that he was on trial for. While she knew he was good for other similar crimes she was able to let it lie until she saw him on the news.

It was another abuse case and his new lawyer also got him off. She was barred from offering information that could have helped regarding prior bad behaviour and that really upset her. As Norie related the facts of the case to me she got increasingly upset. At one point she appeared ready to explode in a rage. When she was done the review, we agreed that we had our next target identified.

He seemed to be your basic businessman, maybe a bit too good looking for his own good. That was about all you could hold against him. Unless of course, you despised men who abused, hit, belittled, or damaged women. This guy was, without a doubt, a serial abuser. When I saw his picture, I knew he was the one I wanted. Once you knew, you could see there was something off about them, usually in their eyes. Sadly, we would have to keep it secret and there would be no opportunity to abuse him like he abused his targets...or would there be?

He worked in the financial world. I thought that was ironic, but it was not the same type of work as Bobby or Jonathon or Luke. It was completely unconnected. He was more of a CFO type of guy although he did not look the part. Norie went into more detail about what he did and how he did it and we both decided it would not be just a simple disappearance. No, there would be a little bit of abuse before we sent him on his own journey to hell.

Norie admitted to me that she not only wanted to see him suffer but wanted to inflict some pain on him herself.

She was a skilled martial artist and even during law school she competed at a high level in both regional and national competitions. This was the first time she had mentioned that. She wielded the bat well when we killed her own husband but that was different.

Almost anyone can swing a bat or punch someone when they are consumed with rage. I recalled the beach episode as she watched me disable two men while she did nothing. I pondered why she had not taken her guy out and figured she just wanted to see how good I was. She didn't quite look the martial arts type, if there was such a thing, but that is likely what made her dangerous.

Like me, Norie was of mixed parentage. Of course, I was the product of a Mexican man and a white woman and she a Japanese woman and a black man. She had a quality to her that was different, and she wasn't the ugliest girl on the planet either. We decided that we would alternate surveillance on this clown, but I was concerned about Norie being spotted. I was of the impression that she would stand out and be memorable in any crowd.

As such, I told her I would handle all the up-close work. Of course, I did not tell her I could do it all from a room in my house that had more spy-power than a CIA office! I now had all his information and I sent Norie home, so I could get to work.

We each had untraceable burner phones that would be our only method of communication from here on out. After she left, I went down to my "office" and got everything set up. John Q. Public was completely unaware but once you had someone's address, name, age and driver's license number you could easily track virtually everything they were doing.

As the days moved forward and I watched him more closely I decided I wanted direct involvement with him. He was currently single, so I started to think up a plan to meet him. That would most likely be the simplest method of getting close to him. I knew which gym he trained at and figured I would join using an alias and then ensure that I was there when he was scheduled. I knew it wouldn't take him long to start chatting me up and I would simply let nature take its course. I talked to Norie about it, and she did not like the plan at all. I explained to her I would be in no danger and that this would be the best way to get him isolated somewhere so we could have some fun.

In the end, Norie agreed with me, and I continued my quest.

The trick to picking up a dirt-bag like this was to not look too eager. Ignoring them a bit always got their attention. It was an affront to their massive ego when any woman ignored them.

I also felt that I didn't want to display my power and strength as that might scare off a serial abuser like him. I'm confident he would not have the cojones to take on someone like me. I had to dial it down a bit. The sad part was that after I was done the girly workout to try to impress him, I would have to go to a real gym to train seriously. I couldn't allow my fitness, endurance or punching power to degrade.

I got some looser clothes that still showed off my body and begin to hit his gym regularly. As I expected, it only took a couple of weeks until he came over and sat next to me on a bike. We had been noticing each other since I started there, the way people loosely connect in a gym. A friendly wave and the odd hello, basic familiarity. I suppose he had now decided I was single, and he was going to test the waters.

He said hi as he got on the bike next to mine and then nothing else until we were done. He got off soon after I did and introduced himself. He extended his hand to me and said, "I'm Robert Stanley." I shook his hand loosely and told him my name was Beth. A nice, middle America understated name that I thought would work. It also matched the fake ID I used to join the club of course!

He moved surprisingly slow, taking another week and a half to ask if I wanted to join him for a bicycle ride.

He said since he saw me spinning all the time, he thought I might be a rider. He was correct of course. I did love to ride.

I said that sounded like a great idea and we arranged to meet in a parking lot at the bottom of the Griffith Observatory road. It was a great ride up and there were trails throughout the canyon that were a blast to ride too. You could easily spend a day pedaling up and down that canyon. You could even get right to the base of the famous Hollywood sign if you worked at it.

At least you could get to the fence that now surrounded the Hollywood sign. Someone had changed Hollywood to Hollyweed a few years back and the solution was to throw up a high fence with razor wire on top. For California, they seemed a little uptight about that incident. I thought it was way too funny but accurate, this place was Hollyweed.

It was a perfect day when we got to the parking lot. Not too hot and a little bit of a breeze. It was an uncharacteristic day for LA this time of year as it would usually be hovering in the nineties. We arrived at almost the same time and proceeded to unload our bikes. He had one of those trendy fat tire bikes and I was quite sure he was not a true mountain biker but that would remain to be seen. I had a killer full suspension bike, so I could ride anywhere, anytime.

He admired my bike when he saw it and commented that it was "a lot of bike, for a woman". I forced out a smile when what I wanted to do was have an in-depth discussion about the stupidity of his comment.

I wanted to race up those hills at a pace I was sure he could not match and then see what he had to say about my bike! I laughed it off and said it was a gift from my father who had lots of money but didn't know a thing about bikes. He was taken advantage of by the bike salesman, and I was now the proud owner of a mountain bike that cost more than my first car. I didn't have the heart to return it, so I kept it.

We had a pretty good day riding up there and then in and around the canyons. It was a decent workout, and he was quite charming. I had to remind myself more than once what a dirty scumbag, woman-hater he was.

We got back to the parking lot, and it had warmed up quite a bit and I had a good sweat going. I couldn't take my shirt off though as I was quite sure when he saw my arms and shoulders, he would likely look for a softer target. I had to keep up the right appearances until he was sucked in, so I left my cycling shirt on.

He asked if I wanted to go for a bite before going home. I said if we sat on a breezy patio that sounded like a good idea. We did, and the day ended well with him hugging me and giving me a light kiss on the cheek.

I was nearly sick but hey, I was a star at pulling men in, so I was confident he figured I was impressed with him.

We went out a few more times and did a few other things. After our last outing I called Norie and told her it was time and asked if she was still in. She said her hands were almost numb from practicing her striking. I laid out the plan. I had rented a remote cabin up close to Big Bear. I used google-earth and a spy satellite to determine it was exactly what we needed. There were very few houses or cabins around and none that were close to this one.

It would be an ideal spot to work for as long as we wanted. There would be nobody to see us go in or out and there was also a canyon close-by where we could easily dispose of the remains. There was just one small road into the cabin off the main road and no lights or road signs close either. I had no idea there were still places this isolated so close to Big Bear.

I used my alias and a pirated credit card number, so I knew that nothing was traceable. We decided it would happen the next weekend. I told Robert I had a surprise for him and that he should bring his bike and meet me at the Griffith parking lot again at noon on Friday. I told him to pack for the weekend so I'm sure he was all horned up on the drive over. It was risky, but I had not yet been to his home and saw no reason to chance it now.

I certainly was not going to have him pick me up at my house either. Separation was key to leaving no evidence behind.

I was excited when the time came to execute our plan. Norie would be up at the cabin before us and would remain hidden in a back room until I told her it was safe. At the appropriate time, she would just step out to "reconnect" with her former client.

I met Robert, we transferred his bike to the jeep I had, and we headed up to the mountains. We chatted all the way and I made my best effort to relax him and have him think he was about to get lucky. In fact, it would be the most un-lucky day of his about-to-be-ended life. By the time we rolled into the driveway at the cabin I could tell he was eager and anxious. He was also completely oblivious to what was about to happen to him.

He was saying how great the terrain looked and how excited he was to get out riding. The cabin was beautiful and much more than it looked on paper. Large, smooth stones made up the whole front of the house surrounded by perfectly shaped cedar beams and posts. The cabin stood as a stark contrast to the forest in which it was hidden but it fit in very well.

I gave him the cabin key and let him go through the door first.

Once he was inside, I disabled him with a blow to the side of the head and he went down in a heap. I muscled him over to a large post that I had completely covered with thick plastic a couple of days earlier. I attached his legs, arms and mid-section to the post with zip-ties and rope and called Norie. She came out looking like she was ready to kill right that second. I calmed her down and told her she needed to take her time and not rush things. She got out of his sight before he came to and waited.

I put a chair in front of him and I sat there waiting for him to awaken. I had no feelings about what I was about to do. In my eyes and in my heart, he was at worst someone who was about to murder a woman, at best he would cause her to die. Either way, I could not let that happen.

He regained consciousness and started yelling at me and saying he was going to kill me when he got loose. I calmly and quietly told him he was not going to get loose, and he had neither the strength nor the skill to kill me. The idiot thought we were going to ransom him or something. Why did this type of guy always think that? Why did they attach so much value to themselves but so little to their spouses?

That was when Norie came over and sat in the other chair. It took him a few minutes, but he eventually recognized her. She smiled at him and said, "you remember me, don't you?"

She said she would be shocked if anyone on this planet thought his life worth saving enough to pay even the smallest ransom. She laughed as she said he was the scum of the earth, and our job was to clean up the garbage.

She explained how sick it made her when he was not convicted and mentioned the name of the other girl he had told her about. She explained to him that even if he would have gone to jail, the rate of recidivism for guys like him was better than 70%. She calmly told him she just couldn't take the chance, so we were going to make sure he didn't hurt any other women. We had no choice.

We knew the state would never give him a lethal injection, but we could make sure he was gone. I had all the usual equipment I would use in a situation where I was trying to extract information before ending someone's life. I had stimulants to bring him back when he was out, IV bags to keep him hydrated, assorted sharp instruments and other tools of persuasion. As I said I was not some sick torturer, but I also knew how to find things out when I needed to. I had a brief twinge of fear that I was beginning to like this part, even though there was no information I needed from him.

It took him a while to shut up but a good stiff shot to the ribs by Norie knocked the wind out of him. I smiled at her as he struggled to suck in a breath. She had pictures of the women he had hurt.

She would hold one up, give him a stiff backhand to the face and then ask, "did you hit her like that?" She must have had at least twenty photos from her files.

Each time she would put a photo right in front of his face and each time she would hit him hard. She certainly had a mean streak. It was obvious she had progressed from being a simple prosecutor to becoming both the person who passed sentence as well as the one who carried it out. We were completely in synch on the whole judge, jury and executioner concept.

We didn't have to worry about leaving any DNA or anything like that as I had a special barrel in the back of Norie's truck that contained my "magic elixir." It was a blend consisting mostly of Sodium Hydroxide (commonly referred to as lye) that could completely dissolve a body in less than four hours. You just had to know the trick to making that happen.

It wasn't good enough to just dump the lye over a body as DNA would remain. It would also take far too long for bones and teeth to dissolve and I'm not sure they would, even given enough time.

Most people thought acids were the answer but with all the bomb-making going on in the world acids are very closely monitored. On the other hand, lye, as in Sodium or Potassium Hydroxide, can be easily and anonymously purchased at farm supply stores. You can get it many places and there are almost no controls on its purchase.

The trick to dissolving a body was that you had to get the lye solution up to a temperature of about three hundred degrees. Naturally, you could not simply put a fire under an open container either or you could blow yourself sky-high.

The drum I used was heavily reinforced and acted like a pressure cooker, which was the only way to get the solution to that temperature. You would put whatever you wanted gone into the barrel, cover it with the solution and then seal it up. Once you got the contents up to temperature, carefully controlling the pressure with a valve, you only had to wait about three to four hours, and it was all over.

When the cycle was complete you were left with a tan colored liquid that resembled mineral oil. In a remote area like this it would quickly disappear into the ground and leave no traces. There would be no body, no evidence, nothing. Just another of the many disappearances that happened in California that would remain unsolved. The kind that makes detectives and special agents crazy!

He was a little bruised and his face was swollen but he had no idea what was coming. I took his face in my hand and squeezed hard, so he could feel my strength. If I wanted, I could simply grab him by the throat and rip out his larynx and windpipe and he would be dead quickly.

That was not our goal so as I held him with one hand, I drove the other fist hard into his side. He coughed and gagged as his flesh and organs absorbed the blow.

He was tied to the pole because his vital organs were exposed, and I knew how to inflict pain without killing someone. Excruciating pain that would have him praying and begging for mercy in no time. I really had intended to soak him down and hook him up to a battery box. One wet sponge on his side and the other to his groin. I can't explain why but I thought that might be crossing a line. I smiled inside as it wasn't like I hadn't crossed a few lines already!

I felt more like some striking practice instead, on a human punching bag, so I stepped back and peeled off my sweatshirt. There was something exhilarating about feeling the crunch of breaking bones or the give in a body shot under my fists. Sure, hitting a heavy bag was good training but there was no feedback. I enjoyed the feedback. Each grunt, groan or whine as the air was violently expelled from his lungs after each blow.

Reactions, breathing, eyes, all telling me how hard and accurate my punch was.

I explained to him that he was the scum of the earth and because the justice system, even with help from my friend Norie, could not save the world from him we would.

His eyes got big as he was finally starting to put two and two together. He began to struggle to try and get free. I knew it was not possible for him to escape and he would soon figure that out.

These were military grade zip-ties, and their tensile strength was into the thousands of pounds. It was impossible for him to get free unless we untied him. We had no plans to do that until we were good and ready to move him to the barrel.

I looked at him and smiled as I got closer. I let loose a vicious six-inch strike into the side of his ribs. I knew it was hard enough to bruise them but not break them and that shot did the trick. He was in serious pain and having even more trouble breathing. I just watched him and smiled as he coughed and fought to suck in even half a breath.

I looked at Norie and asked if she had anything to add. She moved directly in front of him and delivered a lighting quick kick directly to his groin. He threw up immediately. He was doubled over as far as he could get and screaming in pain. He was close to passing out, so we let him experience that feeling for a while.

As he started to recover Norie got in close to him and laughed saying, "I guess those won't be of much use anymore, not that they were much use to begin with."

He tried to head butt her as the top half of his body was loose, but she easily dodged it and then struck him directly in the mouth with a hard uppercut. He was bleeding fairly good, and I was sure she had loosened a couple more of his teeth.

I let him see me casually putting on a pair of leather bag gloves. They are basically very thick leather gloves, usually with a metal rod in the palm that one uses on a heavy bag. I removed the metal bar because with my power, if I did leave the metal bar in, he would be dead with one or two blows.

We didn't want that, we wanted him to live the pain the way the women he abused did. We gave him a few sips of water and then we sat down. "How are you feeling Mr. Robert Stanley?" Norie asked. "Do you think you feel like the women you abused yet." He said nothing, just coughed up a little bit of blood and spat toward us.

I wanted to see fear, so I stood up and got close to him. I had my hand around his throat to prevent another head-butt attempt. I calmly explained that we were indeed going to kill him but added that it was going to take us at least two days to do so. During that time, he would feel unimaginable pain and will have already started begging us to just kill him. I let him know we will continue well past that point and may even just let him live a disfigured and painful life. The look on his face was priceless.

A combination of fear, hate and resignation washed over him like the waves of the ocean settling onto the shores. It had already been a long day, so we gave him another drink, a little protein shake and then we went to sleep for a while. I woke up in the morning feeling completely refreshed and ready to get back to work. I walked out and as I passed him, I slapped him hard in the back of the head.

I said, "wake up jerkoff we have things to discuss." It was sort of like punching into a time clock at the office, or at least it was in our office.

Norie came out a few minutes later and she had some of her martial arts training gear with her. As Robert watched she explained that she couldn't trust herself not to kill him quickly. She added that she was going to put the headpiece on him and the body padding. That way she could hit him as hard as she wanted without killing him. I smiled at her and told her I liked the way she thought. She put the protective gear on him and went to work. It was like she was hitting a training dummy, except with a great deal of power and hate.

I guess she liked the feedback too. Each strike, even though he was padded up, followed by a grunt, groan or air being forced out of his lungs.

I can duke it out with just about anyone, but as far as martial arts go, I had never seen anyone hit another human being so fast and so hard in rapid succession. It reminded me of one of the guys I used to work with. His favorite phrase was, "I hit him so hard and so fast he thought he was surrounded."

I smiled when I remembered him and when he first used that phrase. Aaah, the good old days. I supposed I was partially reliving those good old days now and perhaps that was part of the attraction for me.

When Norie was done he was coughing, hacking and spitting out blood. She took the gear off and said, wow that was more fun than I thought. He was slumped over, and he didn't see her go over to the pool table. She grabbed a couple of snooker balls and dropped them into a thick sleeve that looked like those old tube socks. I had seen this done before but it was a little crude for my purposes. It was a foreign country type thing to do. I think I saw something like this in one of those James Bond movies. They were usually so fake I couldn't stomach them, but I watched that one start to finish. I enjoyed a good action flick every now and then. I even got some innovative ideas from one or two of them.

She spun it around and around and you could hear it whizz through the air as she slowly walked across the room. She stopped twirling it and let it hang by her side as she got closer. I think he figured it out before I did as she moved in front of him and again began to spin the contraption. It went faster and faster with each loop until she brought it up between his legs where it stopped dead.

He screamed a sickening scream as the sleeve and balls dropped back down to her side.

He was yelling and begging her to stop as she started to spin it again. Faster and faster and then a slight adjustment and right up into his groin again. He was convulsing and yelling and crying at the same time. She let him look down and see why he was in so much pain. That was the last thing he saw before he passed out.

I hooked him up to an IV and we took a little rest before we gave him some stimulants to bring him back. We both knew we were not quite finished yet.

Norie said how disgusted she was that she could do this but she was filled with so much rage directed toward Mr. Robert Stanley.

She spat out the words each time she said his name. She always had to use his full name, explaining that she had to refer to him as that throughout the whole trial. It made her sick. I suggested maybe we should finish up, so she can relax for a day before going back to work. We agreed to just a little more before a painful ending to his sorry life. I gave him a little shot of adrenaline and he came to right away, screaming as he came back to us.

Norie asked if she could finish him, so I put the gloves on her and told her to go to work. She obviously knew something about vital organs too. She gave him a few general body shots and a couple to the head. She then unleashed two massive strikes just about where his spleen would reside.

The spleen was protected by ribs and sat about halfway between the shoulders and the glutes on the left side of a person's back.

She knew that a strike where she hit him would drive a rib or two in that would lacerate the organ. The strength of the blow might even make it all the way through to the spleen itself. As I watched him bruise almost immediately, I knew she had blown up his spleen with one of those two shots. There was not going to be too much time left as I knew he was bleeding heavily internally.

Internal was good because it meant less to clean up. We had plastic down everywhere, so cleanup would be quick and easy anyway, but why make a mess if you can avoid it? I was a killer, not a housekeeper. I suppose just to make sure he was really suffering she got close to him and stomped each of his feet. The boots she was wearing combined with the strength of the stomps must have broken at least half the toes on each foot. She said she liked the effect when I did it to her scumbag husband and wanted to try it herself. She really was a mean little one! A bit unhinged at this point, but mostly just mean.

She finally said enough was enough and began to rain blows into his body, alternating from side to side. Each strike knocked more wind out of him, and he was no longer able to scream or make much sound at all. The only sound coming out him was the rush of breath as each powerful strike found its target.

She looked like a boxer standing in front of a heavy bag. Left, right, left, right, left, right over and over. The end came not soon after, with Norie delivering blow after blow that destroyed his nose and face too and shortly thereafter, killed him. We sat back to relax for a few minutes. We agreed it was odd that we felt nothing but contempt for him. We did not regret what we had done because he deserved exactly what he was getting.

We cut the ties, wrapped him up in the plastic and took him out to the barrel. We hoisted him into the barrel and covered him completely with the solution. We sealed the top and then started the propane burner housed in the bottom. In four hours, we would shut it off and then wait for it to cool.

Soon there would be absolutely no evidence that anything happened here except a weekend of mountain biking. We went inside and kicked back with a drink while we waited for the solution to do its work. Once everything was cooled down, we loaded up the drum and drove out to the edge of the canyon. We dug a shallow hole and slowly dumped the oily contents out. We then tossed a few shovelfuls of dirt on top.

We went to a different spot, removed the burner system, buried the barrel in a hole, and covered it over with dirt.

It wasn't quite as good as eaten by sharks, but I knew there would be absolutely no evidence of him left in a couple of days. The barrel would simply rust away over time, safely buried where nobody would find it.

We added all the plastic and other waste into another barrel and dumped some magic elixir into that. There was no need to heat it as the materials and waste inside would dissolve quickly. It wasn't like dissolving teeth, bones and skulls. This was much easier.

As we drove back to town separately, I decided there would be no more torture sessions. We would just go about our work, identify the worst people and eliminate them. I concluded that complete disappearance was both easier and safer than any other method. The simpler the method the less likely were the chances of anything going wrong.

I didn't know how long I could keep doing this, but I had no intention of leaving any clues behind or getting caught. I felt I could go on forever but IF I stopped, it would be my choice. Unlike "typical" serial killers I had no desire for any accolades or glory. This was truly just a job to me, my contribution to making the world a better place.

We spoke on our phones, and we agreed that we would do one more together. I told Norie to pick carefully as this would be my last.

I was worried that I had developed a taste for torture and knew that would eventually give me away. I had to stop for at least a while to break out of that thinking and try to normalize myself.

I couldn't understand why I was unable to stop myself. I had always been level-headed, but I guess everything I did while in Special Forces had more of an effect on me than I originally thought. Maybe it was that whole PTSD thing about which I was always reading. They said it could affect different people in quite different ways.

Some people would go on shooting rampages, some would beat a spouse to death and others would go over the edge if a car back-fired close to them. It was a terrible affliction and one that affects many of our returning troops. As a country, we really need to do more to help these people who put their lives on the line for us and others, sometimes at the whim of politicians.

We agreed we would lay low for a while and that I needed at least six weeks of R & R. I said that I would get in touch, and she should keep her burner phone charged.

Chapter 30 Two – Rest and Relaxation

I could tell that I needed a break. I was starting to do things I had never done. Things that were very out of character for me. I would go back to my usual life, or at least what I had hoped would be my usual life. Surf, sun and sand. I was not doing too well at maintaining the new life I had created and knew I had to work harder at it. It seemed odd that being a normal, laid-back Californian took so much work for me.

Kathy and Angela were used to me disappearing on trips so there were no issues that way. I met up with them at the gym during a workout and we all hugged and said we really need to get together for lunch. We agreed to meet on Thursday at Duke's in Malibu. I wanted to watch the ocean and feel the breeze. On a sunny Southern California day there was just no better place to be than on one of those patios. I always felt at peace and could sit there for hours people-watching and staring out at the waves.

I get a real kick out of going to Duke's in Malibu. It is right close to the pier just like the Duke's in Huntington Beach. Malibu had a unique idea though. The atmosphere was always awesome, but they kicked it up a notch. They have the original Gidget working there.

Kathy Zuckerman is known as one of the 25 Most Influential Surfers in the world according to Surfer Magazine.

She used to surf by the Malibu pier all the time and due to her diminutive stature was given the nickname Gidget by her surf-buddies, meaning girl midget. Not very cool to use that phrase now but back then it was no issue and she thought it was great to have a nickname anyway.

Her father was the one who wrote the original Gidget novel in 1957 using her nickname and daily life as inspiration. The novel spawned movies and TV shows almost immediately. Kathy Z was truly an American icon, and everyone loved her.

She was at the restaurant a few times a week as their "Ambassador of Aloha", as she was named by Duke's. She would always take time to chat with people at almost every table. She is something like 72 years old now, but she has the same personality as back then according to people who knew her in those days.

I was looking forward to seeing her again almost as much as lunch with the girls. I could eat at Duke's once or twice a week if I had the opportunity. Their food was tremendous and the atmosphere there was undeniably California. I loved Duke's seared ahi bowl and, although I tried to order something different, I almost always ended up ordering it. I was bad for that and really needed to break the habit.

I suppose I had a few habits I should try to break.

Thanks to Duke's oceanfront location we all decided to have a little sun on the beach and watch the surfers and paddleboarders before eating. It turned out to be a perfect day and I wished I was on my bike. As I wanted to wear shorts, I decided to take my car instead of my Harley.

I pulled into the parking lot right behind the two girls, laughing as I got out of my car. Good timing, I said. We agreed what a great day it was and went to find a spot to lay in the sun. We laid out towels, took off our shorts and shirts and got busy tanning. If you can call tanning busy!

I noticed a group of guys up the beach checking us out, but I suppose that was to be expected. As I said before, these girls were your total California beach babes. I never felt I could ever fit into that mold. Sure, I knew I looked good in a bikini or my favorite new swimsuit but there were always the questions about the shape I was in. I guess the bottom line is that I often felt out of place with other women. Regular women.

When I was in a bathing suit, I believed people were focused on my muscles. Women, many times, were simply envious of the shape I was in. Guys, more often than not, seemed to see me as a bit of a curiosity. I think many times they assumed I was a lesbian.

Oh well, I was relatively happy with my lot in life, and I certainly preferred to be me over either of them. They were both smart, fun and great to hang around with, but I know they struggled with being minimized because they were both so beautiful.

We had a nice couple of hours in the sun and decided it was time to go in and eat. Besides, I was in need of a margarita soon. We all put on our shorts and went in. None of us saw a reason to put on a top. Our bathing suits kept us covered enough and there was sun to be had on Duke's patio too.

No shirt, no shoes, no service almost never applied to women on the beach anyway. It seemed we could get away with just about anything here in La La Land.

We arrived early enough that we were seated at a nice ocean side booth. The paved path ran right next to the patio. A thin strip of hot asphalt was the only thing between us and the sand and it was a great spot to people watch. Not as good as Venice Beach but still fun. You saw everything from George Hamilton tanned, leather skinned fifty and sixty-year-olds, to grannies on roller blades to girls who were no doubt too young to wear what they were wearing.

Disco betty, who used to rollerblade with a snake around her neck, could only be seen at Venice though. At Venice, Betty was considered mainstream!

There was still a never-ending stream of diversity flowing by on the path at Malibu almost year-round and I enjoyed sitting back and watching it happen.

We ordered our drinks and the girls told me about a big office party they were having that weekend. They said there would be non-office people too and they expected me to be there. I put up not too much of a fight and, of course, ended up accepting. They always knew I would. It was just a fun thing we did now. I would pretend I didn't want to go; they would look all sad and then I would give in after all.

They were kind of like the girlfriends I never had in high school, and I really loved them both. We were just sipping on our first round of margaritas when a familiar voice behind us said, "so, that's what you people do all day." It was none other than Special Agent Colin Sharpe. I had not seen him in quite a while and thought he looked different. He chatted with us for a few minutes and then excused himself as he had a meeting close-by.

Once he was out of earshot, I asked the girls what was up? He had clearly lost weight and he looked tired to me. At the same time, they both had a grave look on their faces and said in harmony, "you haven't heard?"

In unison, they each said they thought the other had told me. I asked what they were talking about, and they said that only about seven weeks ago that Colin's wife, Patti, had died. I was completely shocked, especially when I got the details.

It first appeared she had died from an overdose. Apparently, she had been taking drugs for quite a while, unbeknownst to Colin of course. She wasn't like a drug fiend or anything but had been using Cocaine and MDMA for a while. The coroner discovered she had died from a bad batch. They couldn't be sure if it was on purpose or not, but she said that frequently they might cut it with some other drug to increase the potency. It may or may not have been what they call a hot shot.

The girls went on to explain that Colin said she had been working on a difficult case. They were not sure if there was a connection, but everyone found it odd how she died. Colin was also completely stunned that she had apparently been using drugs for awhile. He didn't really believe that was the case. Sure, he may have missed an abuser living right next door, but he couldn't have missed a drug addict in his own house.

He explained a few weeks ago that she had been working on a case and was close to finalizing a profile on the main suspect. He thought the timing was troubling. She was about to help crack a major case and suddenly she dies from a drug overdose?

Knowing law enforcement guys like I knew them I recognized that Special Agent Sharpe would be going doubly crazy about now.

He had not only lost his wife, someone he obviously loved, but it could also become a mystery that might consume him. Situations like this almost always worked out the same. When it's a police officer involved, they tend to dig and dig and dig until they burn themselves out. There are also those who turn to their own life of crime or simply just descend into the depths of sorrow and never return.

I wondered which one Special Agent Sharpe would end up being? He seemed to be strong, committed and intelligent. I suspected he was most likely to work hard to legally find the people responsible for his wife's death and bring them to justice. I asked if he would be at the party and Angela said he had been out and about and seemed to be doing a few regular things now. She expected we might see him there for at least a short time.

Thankfully, Gidget dropped by our table shortly afterward and that lightened the mood. She was so bubbly, a real natural upper. She always had a happy story to share. Talking about her Dad, surfing or something that happened at the restaurant was what she got paid to do. You knew that when she left you would invariably feel happier than before she arrived. She was a like a completely legal and free high.

I envied people like that. I used to think they were faking it, that nobody could be that happy all the time. Apparently, they could, and Gidget was a living example of that fact. Too often people were a lot LESS alive after I left! Not people I knew and liked though, so I could at least take solace in that fact. I wasn't just another crazy serial killer. I never hurt innocent people, only those most guilty who deserved to die. I, and now we, only targeted those who had slithered through the cracks in the walls of justice.

We had a great lunch and chatted for a couple of hours. Those frosty margaritas were so good. We decided that after we were done that we should walk around for at least an hour or two to wear off some of the booze. It was such a lovely day. I was super happy that I had earned a great pension and my time was my own to do with as I pleased. I didn't have a rich husband, but I didn't fault the girls for that or hold it against them.

We just talked and talked as we walked up and down the ocean front. I could listen to the sound of those waves forever, feeling the warmth of the sun on my skin. Almost without fail, I heard Beach Boys songs in my head during these times. We strolled back to our cars and headed home after a few enjoyable hours at the beach. I cranked the Beach Boys endless summer on my drive home, singing the words of every song like I was Brian Wilson.

Every time I listened to that music, I was transported back to July 1976 at Angels Stadium, even though it happened five years before I was born! I knew my parents were there and they talked about it quite often. It was so easy to see myself in the crowd as I listened to the music and sang along.

The party came sooner than I expected, and my phone rang in the early afternoon, startling me. I had dozed off on my deck. It was Kathy reminding me that it was an early start as Jonathon was trying out some new appetizer recipes. I told her I would be there in a couple of hours and they should save some for me. I showered and got dressed, just pulling on shorts and a light tank top. As usual I had stuff in my bag along with my swimsuit, in case I didn't feel like coming home or consumed a few too many drinks.

I parked out front of their house and rang the bell. I was greeted with big hugs from Kathy and Jon, and we went inside. Jonathon was just gushing about his new appetizers and said I was just in time. He had tried out a new recipe for char-broiled oysters and Kathy and I would be the first to taste them. He was so cute for a rich guy. He seemed to really take pride in discovering or inventing a new recipe. He was a real grill king and I wished I could find a guy like that. Rich, attractive, a great cook and a great guy.

Jon made us each a drink and we all went out to the patio.

We watched as he worked the large grill, spraying something on top of the oysters every now and then. He was keeping a close eye on them as, like always, he wanted them to be perfect.

He brought us four each to start and sat down. He was so anxious for us to try them. I had one first and did my best to make a disgusted face. I was considering spitting it out to mess with him. I couldn't because it was one of the best things I had ever tasted. He looked like he was ready to cry so I came clean and said how delicious it was. He called me a jerk but smiled broadly at my approval.

I asked him what the secret was, and he told me he had discovered it in New Orleans at a waterside restaurant. The server recommended their char-broiled oysters as some of the best. He too decided on his first bite that they were indeed the best he had ever tasted. The server was kind enough to share their secret when he asked.

Turned out that they melted some butter and cheese on the stove, added in pepper sauce and then brushed that over the oysters on the half shell. The trick was that they misted cold water as they sat on the BBQ and that allowed them to cook perfectly from the bottom up. He had added his own spices as well and they really were the best thing I ever tasted. Each bite was an explosion of flavor in my mouth. We begged for more as soon as ours were finished, and they were finished quickly.

I looked at Kathy and said if she ever gets tired of him, I will take him off her hands. They both smiled but I think Jonathon took the comment more to heart. It was cute to see such a successful guy flattered by such an innocuous comment. He really was charming and genuinely fun to be around. He wasn't Gidget, but he was in that ballpark. When Jonathon was around you had a tough time not being happy.

More people started to arrive. Jonathon was in his element, BBQing up a storm of different little snacks and appetizers. Everyone seemed to like everything as usual. He really was an excellent amateur chef.

I stood by the grill with him, and we talked briefly about how the company was doing without Bobby. They said they missed him, but the company didn't miss a beat. They still found it odd he was gone but they weren't dwelling on it, at least at work. They had upgraded their security systems and cameras but other than that it was back to business as usual.

Just then I saw Colin Sharpe coming up the beach as I glanced out at the ocean. I excused myself and said I would be right back. I wanted to catch him alone and tell him how sorry I was for his loss. I felt terrible for him, even though he was sort of my enemy.

The loss of someone close to you at such an early age is always devastating. I understood that better than most.

I stepped off the last step onto the warm sand and as I did, he spotted me. He waved at me, and I waved back as I walked towards him. I got closer and said how sorry I was that Patti was gone. I told him how shocked I was and made a comment about the good ones leaving us too soon.

He thanked me, and I gave him a little hug and said let's grab a beer and relax. It was nothing sexual or anything of course, just one human being consoling another. He looked so dejected and alone. I assumed anger would take over his emotions relatively soon. I had little confidence he would make it to acceptance and hope, but who knows? People can surprise you during times like these.

He seemed to pick up and get livelier when we hit the patio and in no time, there was good music along with lots of food and drink. The day was pretty good and a lot of fun. Unfortunately, it became one of the few times in my life I had consumed too much alcohol and I was a little off. I supposed I was feeling safe with this group and had allowed myself to completely relax. I knew them all well and if I had wanted to share information about my past, I felt I could have done so with them.

I got a little rambunctious, sort of like when I was with my old unit. We used to rip it up fairly good in those days and we frequently ended up wrestling or full-on fighting at some point. I was like the tough big guy they always wanted to try on for size. Except for the fact they were all usually bigger than me. In virtually all cases it was a mistake. The techniques, moves and power were built in to me and so ingrained that even too much alcohol only slightly diminished my effectiveness. I knew I had to watch myself, but I was always just having a lot of fun.

There wasn't a day that passed where I didn't miss those guys. Even though we almost always worked in isolation there were many times we were together before or after work. It was those times, and the feelings of camaraderie, which remained fresh in my mind. That was the reason I missed the teams.

Luke and Angela had showed up and we were all sitting around a table waiting for the next appetizer. Luke made some comment about the shape I was in claiming I looked like I could wrestle. He then started saying how he was a top-flight division 1 wrestler in college. He had won all these medals and championships and that sort of thing.

Since Title IX, everyone seemed to have a position on men's vs women's sports in the NCAA.

Although Title IX was implemented way back in 1972 to drive equality in funding between men's and women's programs, in many ways it was still an uphill battle today. Football always said they were a separate entity because they brought so much revenue into the school. They thought their programs should be viewed as self-supporting and not be subject to title IX.

Male wrestlers were one group of athletes whose ranks were more decimated than others, some replaced by increased funding to women's programs. It would usually be a sore spot, especially in the mid-west schools as they were hit hardest. I mentioned my own college athletic career and joked about watching the wrestlers. I told him how we always thought they should add tutus to their uniforms. He was not impressed with that comment, and he didn't even crack a smile or make a joke. I really wasn't being nasty; it was just something I would have said to the guys back in the old days.

For some crazy reason Angela piped up and said that I could probably beat him now. He was clearly NOT impressed, and he laughed about it, a little too loud for my likes. Angie said it again and he made some stupid comment I would have never expected from him regarding women and men. I laughed back and said he wouldn't be much of a challenge for me and that it would not be a fair fight anyway.

I wished I had not had too many drinks! He kept pushing and egging me on and I finally looked at him and said, "don't blame me when I kick your ass." He laughed the hardest of all at that comment, so I got up and headed toward the sand. "Let's go big boy, show me your college wrestling moves."

He followed me to the sand and came at me with about a quarter effort, if that. He was saying he didn't want to hurt me. I told him he was going to get embarrassed anyway he should at least do it with a full effort as I easily slipped his move. He came back at me with another attempt to take my legs and he ended up with his face in the sand.

I watched him position his feet and I likely knew before he did what he would attempt next. He was going to try and get close, push to one side and then spin to take my back. I let him get about ¾ of the way around, slipped his move and flipped him over my hip by the head. He hit hard on the sand, and I heard a puff of breath. I smiled down at him thinking he might call it off and that would be that.

I saw a little more determination in his eyes as he got up and brushed the sand off. There never seemed to be a clever way for me to get out of these situations. He made some wiseass comment and, even though I shouldn't have, I laughed at him again.

For me, it was just a natural response and usually a terrific way to disarm an opponent. When someone was blinded by rage, they typically lost whatever advantage over me they may have had. I was already tired of the game, and I knew he would not stop so I did my best to let him pin me. He made a textbook move they were taught in high school wrestling, and I was tapping out a minute later. We got up, brushed off the sand and I was ready to head back for a drink.

I would have been fine with that ending except for no sooner were we standing than he was mocking me. Talking about his gold medals and trash-talking me. Before I could stop myself, I said we needed to go two falls out of three to make it real. He seemed to be walking away and then pivoted towards me. He led with his right arm to control my leg.

I slipped underneath him, twisted his arm hard and flipped him around as I got his back. I had him in a solid headlock and if I had wanted to pressure the back of his neck, he would have been out cold in 20 seconds or so. He decided to tap out as he knew I had him and with a scissor lock, using my legs around his midsection. He knew he was trapped.

Surprisingly, he was still yapping. For me it was kind of like being with the guys again. The only difference being there was no way he could even come close to the level of any of the guys I had worked with.

I gave him the option of leaving it at a tie and he said it could not end on a lucky hold. He was proclaiming that he slipped, saying he let me even it up. Man, he sure knew how to push my buttons. If only he knew...

I smiled at him and just said sure, last fall, no rules and no holds barred. The poor fool seemed to think this was a good idea. I certainly had no intention of striking him as carrying him bleeding back to the patio would not look good. I would wait for him to attack and then counter, subdue him, and that would be that.

We squared off and he tried another bush league move on me that I easily avoided. I laughed, and he was suddenly like a charging bull. He thought he was simply going to overpower me. I let him get close and I jumped and spun and before he knew it, I had him in a triangle choke hold. I held his arm tightly as one of my legs went under his other arm and over his chest, meeting my other leg which was behind his neck. He was now completely immobilized with one arm trapped between my legs and his neck and the other arm being pulled towards me.

I told him I would let him go if we never spoke of this again. Surprisingly, he agreed, and I let him up. That was when I noticed we had an audience on the edge of the patio watching us. All the women were clapping and woo-hooing as the guys looked on just a little stunned.

I saw Colin's face in the crowd and immediately got worried I had let something slip. He now had an inkling of what I could do.

Luke wasn't exactly a 98-pound weakling getting sand kicked in his face. He was still in great shape and obviously a powerful man. I knew I had better come up with a convincing explanation for my prowess and quickly.

I was greeted with a round of high fives when we got up to the patio.

Someone asked how I learned to wrestle, and I told them about my four brothers. I pointed out that I had used two illegal moves on a freestyle wrestler and that if I would have stuck to the rules he likely would have won. Luke came over and hugged me and raised my hand in the air and I could tell we were good. He was still shocked, but all was well. I was surprised at how well he accepted clear defeat. Perhaps he was more evolved than the average guy.

I was not so sure I was good with Special Agent Sharpe though. I had nothing but water and soda with lime for the rest of the time. I was genuinely concerned. The party kept on for a while and Colin came over to chat and talk about the "big fight".

He said how impressed he was with my moves and mentioned he knew a lady at the academy who was great at hand to hand. He added that as good as she was he didn't think she would stand a chance against me. I thanked him and said something about a lucky hold.

He began quizzing me on where I learned those moves and asking what I did before again. I ignored the previous occupation question and I told him my brothers were all great at MMA. They had showed me a few moves in case I needed to defend myself on a date. Colin smiled briefly and said that it was always good when a woman could defend herself.

We all chatted and hung out a bit longer and then I excused myself to go up to bed. I went in the room, locked the bathroom door from my side and then locked the bedroom door. I was asleep in no time and slept quite well considering the amount of alcohol I had consumed. I suppose switching to water helped clear it out of my system.

I awakened to bright sunshine streaming in the window and the smell of breakfast coming from the kitchen. Tough to beat the smell of bacon cooking. I padded downstairs and said how great everything looked. Jonathon was in full chef mode already as one would expect. He was the best host.

There was a Denver omelette, some special kind of French toast and all kinds of other food. Luke and Angie had slept at home but came back for breakfast. We chatted a little bit about the party but dismissed the topic of the big fight quickly and without much fanfare.

I explained my brothers and MMA again and that let Luke off the hook. He saved face, and all was well again.

We ate and talked for a couple of hours, enjoying more of Jonathon's cooking. I had my fill of food, thanked everyone and took off home.

Chapter 30 Three – Getting Restless

A few days later I eased out of bed to go for a run. Instead, I just sat there on my faded sofa staring out the window for what felt like hours. It had been almost seven weeks since I had seen Norie. Nothing in the news, no updates from Colin, everything seemed good. I was starting to get anxious though. I wondered if Norie had any second thoughts?

I grew more concerned as I found myself thinking and dreaming of the next target. It was only every now and then and little to no detail the first few times. As we got further and further from what Norie and I did, I had more and more dreams. There was also a lot more detail and included painful, slow deaths in almost every dream. I sometimes would even have a dream about a past mission and how I could have improved it. I began to get worried that I would be unable to stop. Oddly I suppose, I never considered that I would ever get caught.

I decided I would contact Norie the next week. I was planning to wait until mid-week but didn't even make it past Monday. I phoned her on her lunch break. We chatted about the weather, what we had been doing, training stuff. You name it, we discussed it.

Finally, Norie said she had someone of interest. She said she had made a copy of the file with all the key details ready for me. We created a plan for her to get me the file. Mailboxes were always traceable, and we certainly were not going to email it or something stupid like that. I guess she could have simply come to my house, but I preferred this method right now.

I told her to put the papers into a half letter-size, plain brown envelope and carry it in her purse. We agreed on a parking lot between her office and home and set the time. I knew it was unattended and there were no security cameras, plus it was a free lot.

I was parked there and appeared to be checking my phone when she pulled in and parked next to me. I rolled down the passenger side window and we exchanged smiles as she threw the envelope through the window. She drove off immediately and I left a few minutes later. I can't recall why I thought we needed the bad crime movie style exchange of the file contents? We had already been seen together by that point, although not by too many people. I think I just wanted to ensure we were not seen together too often in case she was connected to a murder. She was certainly more exposed than I, but I had to protect myself.

I returned home and laid out the file contents on my kitchen table. There were some gruesome photos along with many notes. The majority of the file contents were privileged lawyer-client communications. Once I was done making my own notes, I would burn these documents completely and flush the ashes.

The more I read, the angrier I became. This guy was even worse than Robert Stanley. To exacerbate the situation, and strengthen my resolve even further, the notes showed that this guy freely admitted to multiple beatings of women. The one he was being tried for with

Norie as his counsel was simply the only one for which he had been caught.

He completely understood the legal system, double jeopardy rules and how to testify on his own behalf. There was no way the legal system was EVER going to nail this guy. He was just too smooth.

What made Norie crazy, was this guy was an accomplished and pathological liar. As a lawyer, even for a scumbag like this, she knew there were questions she could not ask him on the stand. If she suborned perjury her license to practise law could be revoked. Her trial preparation was meticulous as usual and even though the prosecutor put on a persuasive case, this dirt-bag roamed free at the end of the trial.

He had successfully convinced the jury that his wife was doing this as part of a messy custody battle. Normally you would not put a guy like this on the stand for fear of him opening the door for the prosecution by introducing an unknown fact. Prosecutors would then jump all over the guy and the fifth amendment was usually forgotten.

Norie didn't want to put him on the stand but for a different reason. She knew he was an accomplished deceiver, and he was intelligent and calm enough that he would make the prosecutors look useless. Of course, he forced her to allow him to testify on his own behalf. His performance was Oscar-worthy. He charmed the female jurors with his mannerisms and good looks and connected with the males according to each personality.

She was sickened as she watched the jury move one by one into his corner. It was plainly obvious, as he maintained eye contact with each juror in turn and explained how the prosecutors were wrong. In the end, the jury believed the lies and skilfully crafted half-truths and Norie won the case.

In this case there was no killing of the wife after the trial. When Norie saw the trial was going to go the wrong way she had set up to have the wife and kids removed from the home and secreted away. At first the wife was skeptical, after all this was her husband's lawyer. Norie knew she could easily get disbarred for doing this, but she just could not allow another woman to be hurt or die because of her.

She had planned to have them move to a different city and was going to use the money she had received from her client to set her up. Of course, nobody could know how it was going to work. On the day of the move she was shocked to receive a call from her guys telling her the wife had changed her mind. She had been in contact with her husband, and they had agreed to reconcile.

He spouted the usual "I'm getting help" and "I'll never touch you again" lies and she was sucked right back in. Norie was beside herself with anger and vowed she would not let this go.

Chapter 30 Four – Igor Must Die

Norie knew this would not end well. These guys NEVER just stopped. They might stop for a brief period, but it never lasted. They usually just got more psychological and better at hiding bruises. They would always learn where and how to hit a woman. In some cases, as children, they learned from watching one parent abuse another. In others, the ideas came from movies and people outside their home. The bottom line was that they were never held to account for their bad behaviour. Norie and I would most certainly hold him accountable and make him pay with his life.

I was only halfway through the file, and I had already decided that Igor was going to meet his maker. I had to chuckle when I saw his name for the first time. The meaning of Igor in Russian is "Warrior of peace." It was taken from the Scandinavian name Ingyar, meaning Ing's Warrior and Ing was the Norse god of peace and fertility. You could not have picked a worse name to describe this guy's character. I wanted to come up with a more accurate nickname for him. Perhaps Norie and I would chat about that? I might favor Alastor which, in Greek, means tormentor or persecutor. That made much more sense to me.

I made my notes and sat on my balcony as I completely burned the file contents in a small trashcan.

Once that was complete and cooled, I went into the washroom and flushed the ashes. I went back inside and phoned Norie, so we could chat about a plan.

She said she was aware that he was again hitting his wife. She also knew the emotional torture was almost as bad as the physical for her. She knew his wife felt trapped and unable to leave. Norie knew exactly what this poor woman was feeling, she had the same feelings herself not that long ago. Sure, she could sue for half of everything and would certainly get it, but that would make him nuts. Norie knew that we were this poor woman's only option. We had no choice but to help her.

She went on to say there was a twist. During the trial she had told the wife she should consider taking out as large an insurance policy as she could on her husband. She was to be the beneficiary and if she were gone it would go to her kids. Norie told her this was standard in many cases, and she casually introduced the concept. Norie said it was basic financial planning and suggested she speak with her financial guy or insurance broker.

The wife said there was no way he would agree and Norie explained the rules on insurance policies. One could take out an insurance policy on someone else's life without telling them. All you needed was to demonstrate that you had a pecuniary interest in them.

In the case of husbands and wives there was clearly a financial component. If one died the other's life would be significantly affected in a monetary way.

They would lose half of the support system required to raise children. That meant you could quietly take out a policy on that person without them ever knowing. Tanya had done just that and was the proud beneficiary of a two-million-dollar life insurance policy on her husband. The incontestability phase was now over as the policy was already three years old and incontestability generally ended after two years, one year in some states. Norie explained that the policy was now payable in full upon the death of Igor. She added that if he died by accident the payout amount doubled.

I didn't know much about insurance so Norie advised that things like dangerous activities and illegal activities would void the policy. Now that the incontestability period had lapsed it would pay out even if there was a suicide. Suicides were always red flags for insurers though and if they decided to come after you, they came hard.

It would be a challenge to make a death like this be ruled suicide anyway. There was a fraud clause that was standard but as Tanya would have no idea what was happening, she could never be convicted of fraud. Policies like this were taken out on spouses all the time. The insurance companies always took a close look at circumstances, but Norie had no doubt at all this one would pay when our work was done.

After the trial she had told Tanya to be sure she did not go to an emergency room or call the police unless she thought her life was in danger. Norie wanted to avoid any record of him continuing to beat her. If she were able to heal herself without police or hospital visits it could be argued that he had actually reformed. That would make him one of the precious few who learned that what they were doing was very wrong.

There would be little reason to dig deeper into his upcoming death if the motive for killing him was removed.

Okay, it was going to be a good old-fashioned accident then. The body would need to be found to ensure a payout was made as soon as possible after the death. A car crash was the most likely option. I would wait until he had just gassed up a full tank and hopefully was headed out on the highway. I used the information Norie had provided to set up all the surveillance I would need. I required at least four weeks to track all his movements and build his schedule. I set up traps on his cellphone, laptop and desktop computers and even monitored his work email. I would watch, wait and build the plan as the facts presented themselves.

I was not at all surprised when, during the first week of surveillance, I learned he had a girlfriend on the side. Guys like this were such dogs. I suddenly could not wait to watch him burn on the earth for a little while, before we sent him to hell to burn forever.

The girlfriend might make it a little more difficult as it could be a challenge to get him alone. I began in person surveillance once I had his schedule confirmed.

He liked to visit his girlfriend a couple of times a week. I watched, not too closely, as he left his office and went for his non-conjugal visits. He was likely telling his wife he was working late or some other lame lie. Cheaters were never all that innovative with their stories I had found.

On the first night I followed him as he drove through the city directly to her apartment. I parked a safe distance away after he did and sat there to watch his car. I hoped these visits were not overly lengthy! He had arrived around 7:00 PM and the sun was already down when he left. I was extremely pleased to see that he drove South down the Pacific Coast Highway to get home. I immediately began hoping that was his usual route as that would simplify the task at hand.

There were many areas with curves and cliffs to stage a car crash on this section of highway. The Southbound lane had many choices of steep cliffs, so it would be much easier to stage an accident. It was the lane closest to the ocean so there wasn't much distance to get over the edge and have the car crash hard onto the rocks far below.

I nailed down his girlfriend schedule and gave Norie a call with my plan. I thought it would be safest to steal a vehicle, change the plates, decal it up and use that. It would need to be a one-ton pickup truck with one of those larger extended bumpers. They looked kind of like the racks on the front of police cars. I realized that it might not happen the first night though and driving around in a stolen truck was a little too dangerous. I would have to buy one to ensure we could complete our task.

I went back to the good old car selling books and Craig's list and started scouting for the right vehicle. It only took me a few days and test driving three trucks to get the right one. We agreed on the price and after doing a lien check I returned with cash. Of course, I had my fake driver's license and was wearing my blond wig and extra clothes along with the glasses. He was happy to sell the truck and I was glad too. It was black with all blacked out trim and even a black bumper guard. It was old enough you could shut the lights off completely so at night it would be close to invisible.

I got it home and put it in my garage. I had to check it over and ensure it was in decent shape. I removed the loud pipes he had on and installed the quietest exhaust system I could find. I also swapped the darkened back window out for clear glass. It would make me just a little closer to invisible as I came up on Igor at night. He likely would not see me until a second before he was plunging over the cliff to a fiery death on the rocks below.

I drove the route a few times to ensure I had options. My obvious preference was to have the road almost deserted. That would be tough and might require three or four trips. Norie would follow behind me in her car for a couple of reasons. First, she could slow the traffic down as he approached the kill spots to hide my work. Second, she could pick me up right away if required.

Our plan was shaping up as I recorded the four best spots to stage the crash into my GPS. It was set to warn me about 500 yards before each corner. That way, I could see if there were vehicles coming the other way and prepare. I would advise Norie via our radios to start slowing traffic down well in advance of the chosen corner. The Pac highway was a difficult road to pass on, especially as one approached these areas so that would make her task easier. The road snaked along the edge of low cliffs abutting the ocean for miles. There were plenty of dangerous curves.

Each night we both donned our disguises as an extra precaution. I had to match my driver's license so wore my blond wig, glasses and the clothes that made me look heavier. Norie's was a little more basic, but it still worked. We took four long and boring trips up and down that highway, following at a safe distance after he left his girlfriend's house. The road was emptier than I expected it to be, but the right opportunity had not yet presented itself. I suppose, once the sun had set there weren't too many reasons to drive it. It was only two lanes and usually slow going. One could get around much quicker using the freeways.

We used these times to test out our two-way radios as well. I had them each equipped with an earpiece. They were more military leftovers from my old employer. They had built in scramblers and an automatic in-conversation frequency changing software. As you carried on a back-and-forth conversation the two units would each change to other random frequencies in synch. Even if, by some wild chance, someone heard anything they would hear only one side of a conversation and it would be garbled. The units would then select a different frequency at random and the conversation could continue.

The fifth time was the charm. He even helped by leaving a little later than usual and gassing up his car on the way. He had no idea how much he was contributing to his own demise. I knew when that car crashed onto the rocks far below it would explode and be immediately engulfed in a firestorm of fury. Nobody could survive that type of wreck.

There would be just enough left of him to enable a solid identification of the charred remains using DNA or dental records. A real crispy critter as the boys used to say. I was confident they would need to go to the dental records for this one but that only took a little longer.

We came up on the first two spots and there was traffic coming the other direction, so we did nothing.

In anticipation, Norie had slowed a couple of cars down behind her. I was glad to see them pass her and fly by me on a straightaway before the next opportunity. I was watching the road ahead and Norie said there were no cars behind her at that point. I told her we were about four hundred yards from the next spot and prepared myself. I scanned the road ahead and behind as we got closer and closer to what would be the point of impact.

I would need to catch him right as he began to turn his wheels to negotiate the corner. His wheels would hit the narrow gravel shoulder already turning which would support evidence of it being nothing more than another single car crash. His car would bounce around on the rocks like a pinball before it blew up and erupted into a towering inferno of revenge and freedom for his wife.

I felt safe there would be no evidence of my coaxing his vehicle over the edge. It would appear as if another guy just dozed off at the wheel and went over the cliff after one drink too many. That was exactly what I wanted. Simple evidence and a relatively quick insurance payout for the grieving widow. I spoke to Norie one more time and everything was still clear. I told her to slow down a bit as I prepared. He was obviously not paying attention to his rear- view mirror, although I felt I was close to invisible anyway. As my GPS ticked down to one hundred yards, I began to slowly close the gap between our vehicles. I eased closer and closer to his bumper and at just the right moment I gunned the truck hard and contacted his car.

I could not have done it any better if I tried another 100 times. The truck pushed his back end smoothly and as I gunned the motor his vehicle was driven through the guardrail directly ahead. I turned my own wheels hard, so I didn't go over too. I was still on the pavement thanks to the narrow road, so any tire marks would blend in with all the others.

The only marks visible were his front wheels turning hard on the gravel shoulder as he crashed through the flimsy guardrail. That would further solidify the "asleep at the wheel" cause of the crash. I chuckled to myself that the only reason it was all so easy was because Igor wasn't satisfied just hitting his wife. He had to have a piece on the side too. I decided the more men I saw outside the forces, the less I liked them.

I parked the truck on a turnout, and I jumped into the car. We drove back to confirm. I had seen the explosion in my rear-view mirror and Norie said it was a massive fireball when she passed. We drove to where we could see the spot from the road and looked down the edge to see if there was any movement. The flames were illuminating the whole area now and it made it easy to scout for a body outside the car. We couldn't see anything, even with the flames illuminating the surrounding rocks.

The flames had diminished by the time cars started going past us and nobody seemed to notice anything. Now that the flames were lower, I could use my night vision binoculars to confirm he was still in the car. I crouched next to our car and switched on my goggles. Thanks to the angle the car had settled at I was able to get a view of the driver's seat clearly. I smiled when I saw one crispy critter in the driver's seat. I gave Norie the thumbs up and she smiled broadly back at me.

We got back into the car, Norie took me to the truck, and we went our separate ways. I drove home calmly, following every traffic law. Shortly after that I pulled into my garage with a sense of accomplishment. I was content in the knowledge that woman's pain would now end. As a bonus, she would have plenty of cash to happily live the rest of her life.

And, I had a great new truck! Always wanted one like this. A big, manly truck, all blacked out and jacked up. I decided I would put the loud exhaust back on as it reminded me of my bike a bit.

I went into the garage the next morning and did a little truck inventory. I took off and did some accessory shopping at the truck store and returned to my garage loaded with boxes. I removed and disposed of the large brush guard bumper and installed a more regular looking one.

I swapped out all the parts to be replaced with better ones, put the old ones in the boxes and threw everything into the box of the truck.

It was a great day for a trip to the dump.

I phoned Norie the next day and told her I needed some time off. I said that she should relax, recharge and focus on work and that I would get back in touch. I did still want to hear from her when the insurance company settled and find out how Igor's widow was doing. I told her after that it would likely be a year before we were back in business.

She sounded disappointed, but said she understood. I will admit to feeling a little sad when I hung up the phone. I was conflicted as to whether it was Norie I would miss the most or our "work". I was still not sure I could stop but felt I had to at least make an attempt.

I received a phone call about a month and a half later. Igor's wife had been in touch with her about something to do with his will. Thanks to the accidental death she was now four million dollars richer and living in a mortgage free house happily with her kids.

I hung up the phone feeling I had earned a rest but wondering how long I could suppress my urges...I decided I would do my best to live the Southern California life I thought I had wanted. It was my only option right now.

In case you were wondering, Abaddon is a name whose meaning in Hebrew translates to Angel of Death. Abaddon was also the king of the locust army in the New Testament.

Keep an eye on my Facebook page C.C.Chamberlane (@ccchamberlane)

You may also contact me directly at CCChamberlane@gmail.com

Other Books from C.C.Chamberlane

SAMAELA: Follow Meg Hernandez as she avenges the death of a friend by attacking directly at the cartel that caused her death. After a year off, Megan decides she needs to get back at it. This time she will be tracking and eliminating drug criminals and she will have a very surprising new partner.

The First Female Navy SEAL: the story of Megan's ascent to the top of the male-only ranks of the Navy SEALs. Find out how she became the machine she is and read about her success at being the best of the best.

SAVING UKRAINE – Meg gets asked to do some jobs for her old boss and then is given the most important mission of her life. She and a few of her old SEAL teammates need to stop the invasion of Ukraine the only way they know how. Cut off the head of the snake and prevent WW3.

Don't miss out!

Visit the website below and you can sign up to receive emails whenever C. C. Chamberlane publishes a new book. There's no charge and no obligation.

https://books2read.com/r/B-A-JWSR-FNUVB

BOOKS 2 READ

Connecting independent readers to independent writers.

Did you love *Abbadon*? Then you should read *Saving Ukraine*[1] by C. C. Chamberlane!

[2]

As a Navy SEAL, Megan Hernandez had completed many critical and dangerous missions. Although she is now a former SEAL, the Secretary of the Navy had contacted her to complete some crucial tasks that included rescuing kidnapped children and then helping to eradicate the threat of Somali pirates.

Those situations handled, she was now being tasked with the greatest and most important mission of her career. A country was being invaded at the whim of its most dangerous neighbor. The cold war had ended years ago and no world event had brought us closer to World War 3 than this disgusting abuse of power. Ukraine was being

---

1. https://books2read.com/u/mYyjoG

2. https://books2read.com/u/mYyjoG

invaded and although they are fighting bravely, the USA simply can not allow the bear to continue its onslaught.

Megan and two of her former teammates are going to remedy this situation and hopefully get out alive. There could be absolutely no evidence or indication that the USA was behind this and she had no idea exactly who within her own government knew of this plan. That did not matter to them because SECNAV needed them and so did the world.

Also by C. C. Chamberlane

Megan Hernandez
Samaela
The First Female Navy SEAL
Saving Ukraine

Standalone
Abbadon

About the Author

C.C.Chamberlane has been a novelist for a few years now. His first series of books include; ABBADON, SAMAELA, the First Female Navy SEAL and Saving Ukraine.

These stories focus on Megan Hernandez and her power and commitment to do good in the world.

www.ingramcontent.com/pod-product-compliance
Lightning Source LLC
Chambersburg PA
CBHW031338020726
47499CB00005B/1315